MY HOME
IS OVER JORDAN

Also by Sandra Forrester
SOUND THE JUBILEE

MY HOME
IS OVER JORDAN

Sandra Forrester

LODESTAR BOOKS
Dutton　New York

Library of Congress Cataloging-in-Publication Data

Forrester, Sandra.
  My home is over Jordan / Sandra Forrester.—1st ed.
    p.   cm.
  Sequel to: Sound the jubilee.
  Summary: No longer a slave now that the Civil War is over, fifteen-year-old Maddie dreams of getting an education and becoming a teacher, but she finds the reality of freedom harsh.
  ISBN 0-525-67568-X (alk. paper)
  1. Afro-Americans—Juvenile fiction. [1. Afro-Americans—Fiction.   2. Reconstruction—North Carolina—Fiction.
3. North Carolina—History—Fiction.   4. Prejudices—Fiction.]
I. Title.
PZ7.F7717My   1997
[Fic]—dc21   97-15591   CIP   AC

Published in the United States by Lodestar Books,
an affiliate of Dutton Children's Books,
a member of Penguin Putnam Inc.,
375 Hudson Street, New York, New York 10014

Published simultaneously in Canada
by McClelland & Stewart, Toronto

Editor: Rosemary Brosnan   Designer: Dick Granald

Printed in the U.S.A.
First Edition
10 9 8 7 6 5 4 3 2 1

In loving memory of my mother,
who taught me to love stories
and inspired me to tell my own

Preface

After nearly four years of fighting, the Civil War ended when the South surrendered on April 9, 1865. The war had taken a terrible toll on this country. More than 600,000 Union and Confederate soldiers had lost their lives, and many others suffered from illness and permanent disability. Civilians, too, had endured hardship, both in the North and the South; but the defeated South, where most of the battles had been fought, was physically and economically devastated.

When the war ended, the South was a wasteland of ash and rubble. Bridges and railroads had been destroyed, plantation houses looted and burned. With no crops to sell, and no money to rebuild their homes or buy seed for planting, white Southerners faced a bleak and uncertain future.

The end of the war also meant the realization of a cherished dream by the four million men, women, and children who had been held in slavery. They were finally *free!*—free to leave the plantations and begin new lives wherever they chose. But they, too, faced great hardship. Because it had been illegal to teach slaves to read, only ten percent of the former slaves could read and write. Most had spent their lives laboring in the white man's fields and had no other work skills. But with the plantation system and the South's economy in ruin, there was little work for the newly freed slaves.

Many Southerners—both black and white—had no idea how or where they would live. They had no choice but to take to the roads. In oxcarts, wagons, and on foot, they began the search for jobs, for loved ones displaced by the war, and for a place to call home.

While poverty and lack of employment made life hard enough for the former slaves, even more difficult was the prejudice they faced. Confused and frightened by the overwhelming changes in their lives, many white Southerners reacted with anger to the freeing of the slaves and blamed them for their own misfortunes. Their hostility was often expressed as harrassment and physical attacks on the former slaves and their property. Blacks were routinely insulted and threatened. Their houses and churches were burned, their animals slaughtered. Some were brutally beaten and killed for no other reason than the color of their skin.

Although the nation was technically at peace, the horrors of bloodshed and destruction did not stop with the end of the war. The fires of vengeance still raged across the South, and the shadow of slavery would follow black Americans into the next century. But the first step toward freedom and full citizenship had been taken, and there was no turning back.

MY HOME
IS OVER JORDAN

1

The wagon rattled slowly down the road behind two aging, skinny-hipped mules. Maddie followed in the tracks of the wagon wheels, mud splattering the hem of her skirt and sucking at her bare feet as she walked. She could have ridden in the wagon bed with her sister and brother, but after days of being pitched and tossed whenever the wagon hit a bump, wading through the mud didn't seem so bad.

"Maddie, can I walk with you?" Pride called from the wagon, where he was nestled among bundles of clothing and bedding.

Mama was sitting on the wagon seat next to Royall. She turned around and felt Pride's forehead. "Lay down and rest—don't want the fever comin' back."

Pride's handsome brown face turned fierce. "That's all I been doin' since we left the island. I'm lots better, Mama."

" 'Cause you been doin' like I say," Mama said, not bothering to turn around again.

"Pride, read to us from your *McGuffey's Reader*," Angeline said to her brother. She was wedged in between Pride and Mama's best rocker. Baby Elizabeth slept in her arms.

"Don't wanta read," Pride muttered. "Wanta walk."

1

He kicked hard at the side of the wagon, and the noise woke Elizabeth. She started to cry.

Angeline frowned at Pride. "You're too big to be havin' hissy fits," she said and began to comfort her baby.

Angeline was right, Maddie thought, as she studied Pride's sullen face. At seven, he was too old to be sulking when he didn't get his way. But he was the only one of Mama's sons to live past infancy, and Mama had always been easy on him. After nearly losing him to the fever last winter, they had all babied him.

Royall looked back at Pride. "You wanta drive the wagon a while?"

Pride's face lit up. As he scrambled over bundles to reach the wagon seat, Angeline smiled at her husband and shook her head. Royall winked at her. Then he pulled Pride into his lap and handed the boy the reins.

They had been on the road for five days now, leaving the coastal sandhills far behind as they moved into the heart of North Carolina. Thickets of oak, hickory, and sweet gum closed in on either side of the road, their dense leaves shading the travelers from the hot May sun. After three years on the tiny island that had been their refuge during the war, Maddie felt overwhelmed by the towering trees and the endless stretch of forest. Mama said they were going to buy a farm and finally have a home of their own, but this silent, overgrown land seemed lonesome to Maddie, not like home at all. She missed the island. And more than anything, she missed her papa.

Maddie felt an ache inside, remembering Papa. His quick smile and the feel of his calloused hand on her

2

cheek. If Papa were here now, she wouldn't be afraid of leaving the island. She wouldn't be afraid of anything because Papa was brave. While the other plantation slaves had waited for the army to set them free, Papa had planned how they would run away from Master and Mistress. He'd seen them safely to Roanoke Island and joined the Union Army to fight for their freedom. Papa had known he might die, but that hadn't stopped him. "Can't 'spect the army to do all our fightin' for us," he had said the day he and Royall signed up. Maddie had known he was right, but still she was afraid for him. And when he hadn't come back, she had known she would never feel completely safe again.

As the wagon rounded a bend in the road, Maddie caught sight of Zebedee up ahead. He had gone on to "do some scoutin'," he said, but Maddie figured he was just tired of poking along with the rest of them. Zeb had shot up tall in the two years since Mama and Papa had taken him in, but he was still skinny as a willow branch. Fifteen now, same as Maddie, Zebedee thought he was a man. But Maddie reckoned his growing hadn't caught up with his thinking.

The sun was beginning to sink behind the trees when Maddie saw Zebedee trotting back toward the wagon. "Cabin up ahead!" he called to them.

The cabin had stood empty for a long time. One end of the roof sagged under the weight of pine needles and dead tree limbs. The chinked walls were barely visible through a tangle of Virginia creeper and sumac.

"Don't look safe," Mama said as she climbed down from the wagon. "Roof's about to cave in."

Royall helped Angeline out of the wagon and took

3

Elizabeth from her. "Reckon we can sleep under the stars one more night," he said.

Zebedee built a fire while Maddie drew water from the well. Soon Mama had a skillet of corn cakes baking.

"How much farther you figure we'll have to go?" Angeline asked as she poured up the last of the buttermilk.

Royall threw some sticks on the fire and shook his head. "Till we find land to buy. Soil on the coast weren't good for farmin'—too sandy." He squatted down and scooped up a handful of damp earth, being careful to keep his bad leg straight. "But this here's good soil for cotton. See how rich it is?"

"No cotton," Mama said.

Royall turned to look at her. "What's that, Miz Ella?"

"I said, we won't be plantin' cotton," Mama said. "My Titus spent his life in cotton fields, and I won't have my son and daughters doin' the same. Like in the slave times. We can grow anything you want, Royall, 'cept cotton."

"Good cash crop," Royall began, then stopped when he saw Mama's face. "But I reckon there's other crops that'll make us money."

After everyone else was asleep, Maddie lay on her quilt staring up at the night sky. There was a big, bright star that she looked for each evening. Miz James, her teacher on the island, had said it was the North Star, but Maddie always thought of it as Papa's star. Sometimes, when she needed to talk to him, she'd go outside and look up at his star and tell him what was on her mind. But tonight, she just stared at the star's cool light until her eyelids grew heavy and she drifted off to sleep.

Sometime later, Maddie awoke with a start. In the

4

moonlight, she could make out the quilt-covered shapes of Angeline and Royall beside her. Wondering what had awakened her, Maddie listened, but the only sound she heard was the mournful call of a whippoorwill. Then she saw movement at the edge of the woods. Someone was emerging from the shadow of the trees into the moonlit clearing.

Maddie's heart beat hard against her ribs. She could make out three forms coming slowly toward the camp. The careful way they moved told her they were up to no good.

She reached across Angeline to wake Royall. He mumbled something when Maddie pulled on his sleeve. Then he jerked awake and sat up, still groggy.

Maddie covered Royall's mouth with one hand and pointed with the other. She felt his body tense when he saw the figures moving toward them. Fully awake now, he patted her arm and slid into the shadow of the wagon. Maddie saw him grab the old rifle he had brought home from the army and creep around the front of the wagon, where he was lost in darkness.

The figures came closer. Maddie was breathing so hard she felt dizzy. As the intruders reached the end of the wagon bed, her eyes searched frantically for a weapon. She seized a lantern—and its rusty handle creaked under her hand.

One of the figures spun toward her. Maddie froze. In another second, she would have flung the lantern at the men, but then she heard the click of metal and Royall's calm voice saying, "Don't move. I got a gun pointed at you."

Maddie kicked the quilt aside and lit the lantern. The others were waking up now. Angeline cried out in alarm when she saw three strangers only feet away from her bed.

"Sweet Jesus," Mama murmured.

"It's all right," Royall said, his rifle still aimed at the intruders' backs. "Now, you men turn around—real slow. Maddie, bring that light over here."

Maddie did as Royall said. She held the lantern high so that it shone into the faces of the men who had frightened her so—only she could see now that they were hardly old enough to be called men. The faces that stared back at her were soft and brown—the rounded faces of boys. And they looked terrified.

Royall peered at them. "How old are you?" he asked the tallest boy.

"Don't know," the boy muttered.

"Couldn't be more'n twelve or thirteen," Mama said. She came closer. "Why you creepin' into our camp in the middle'a the night? You goin' to rob us?"

The boy nodded. Maddie saw that he was trembling.

"Well, least he don't lie," Royall said sharply, but he didn't look angry. "What wuz you gonna take?"

"Food," the boy said.

Mama's face softened. "You hungry then?"

"We ain't eat in two days."

"Where's your folks?" Mama asked.

"Don't got none." The boy had stopped trembling. He looked Mama straight in the eye. "The master sez to us we's free, and we's some more happy 'bout that. Then he tells us to get off his land—takes his gun and shoots in the air and sez *git!*' Only we don't have nowheres to go and there ain't no work. Ain't no food, neither."

6

Mama studied the boy's face and nodded. "Zebedee," she said, as she reached for the coffee pot, "build up the fire. Maddie, get the corn cakes left from supper."

They sat around the fire while the three boys gulped down hot coffee and had their fill of corn cakes and fried apples. At first, they crammed the food into their mouths as though they couldn't get enough. When they had slowed down some, Mama started asking questions.

"How long you been on the road?"

The tall boy, who was called John, wiped his mouth on his sleeve. "Near a month," he said.

"How you been livin' all that time—stealin' from folks?"

John ducked his head, and the other two never looked up from their food.

Mama sighed. "Never mind," she said. Then, "You mean to say there's no work a-tall around here?"

"No work for slaves," John said.

"Ain't no slaves no more," Royall said. "You're free—same as a white man."

The boy cut his eyes at Royall. "Then how come I don't see my master on the road starvin'?"

Before they left, Mama packed up some hard biscuits and bacon. When she handed the bundle to John, he smiled for the first time. "Much obliged," he said softly.

"You seem like good boys to me," she said, looking at each of them for a moment. "Good boys goin' through hard times. But bein' hungry don't give you the right to steal from other folks. 'Sides which, you could get yourselves killed. What if Royall had fired without botherin' to get to know you?"

7

"So what's we s'posed to do?" John demanded. "We ain't got no money. How's we s'posed to eat?"

"You catch fish, hunt rabbits, do day work for a hot meal. You do whatever you got to, but you don't creep in on folks at night and scare 'em half to death," Mama said firmly, "and you don't take what don't belong to you."

As they set out on the road, Mama called after them, "I mean it, now. You do what's right. Even if it's hard, you do what's right."

Maddie and Zebedee walked together behind the wagon. There was silence all around them except for the creak of the wagon wheels, the occasional cry of a bird, and the discordant sounds of Pride learning to play the harmonica.

"What you think it'll be like?" Zebedee asked suddenly.

"What will *what* be like?"

"The farm we's gonna buy."

Maddie pondered this. "I reckon it'll be small," she said finally, "with the money we got to buy it."

"We got most'a Royall's and your papa's army pay."

"Never *did* get all'a Papa's pay." The words came out sounding harsh, but she didn't need to cover up how she felt. Not with Zeb. " 'Course, we're better off than some. Sula's family never saw a cent'a her papa's pay."

"Don't seem right," Zebedee said. "Our men wuz soldiers same as the whites—bled the same and died the same." Then he stopped, a stricken look on his face. "Maddie, I never meant it to come out that way."

"No harm done," Maddie said softly. But the ache left by Papa's dying seemed to grow a little.

As they walked on, Maddie felt Zeb watching her anxiously out of the corner of his eye. Maddie knew he was trying to figure out how to ease the hurt he feared his words had caused. She looked up at Zeb and smiled. When he saw that, the tension drained from his face and he grinned at her.

"You know, Maddie Henry, sometimes I think on what woulda happened to me iffen I hadn't made it to Roanoke Island," he said. "Never knew what a family wuz 'fore I met the Henrys. Once I got to know y'all, it woulda took the whole Union Army to make me walk away."

Late that afternoon, as they reached the Tar River, Royall pulled the wagon to a halt.

"Why we stoppin'?" Zebedee called to Royall.

"Come see for yourself," Royall said.

Joining him and Mama at the front of the wagon, Zebedee and Maddie looked down at the swiftly moving waters of the Tar. Once, a bridge had spanned the river, but all that remained of it were bits of charred wood along the steep banks.

Early on in their journey, they had passed fire-blackened chimneys standing alone amidst piles of ash and loose brick. Crops had been burned and fences destroyed. Even though Royall had told them this was part of war, and it was war that had led to their freedom, the sight of those charred ruins had sickened Maddie. She looked now at the burned-out bridge and felt that same awful churning inside.

"We can't cross here," Royall said. "Water's too deep."

"Reckon there's another bridge?" Angeline asked.

"Either way, it's gettin' close to sunset," Mama said. "We best be lookin' for a place to camp."

"There's a house over yonder, through them trees," Royall said. "Maybe they'll let us draw water." He clucked to the mules and turned the wagon onto a weed-choked trail that ran along the riverbank.

The plantation had been beautiful once. Maddie could see that as the trail widened and wound through a rusted iron gate. At the end of the trail, the house rose three stories from a brick foundation. Its once-white walls were weathered silver, and most of the window glass was gone.

The only sound that greeted them as they passed under tupelo gums and giant elms was the buzz of insects. No human or animal stirred on the place.

Then Maddie saw the all-too-familiar sight of burned wood. Behind the house, where barns and stables and storehouses should have stood, were the grim, blackened reminders of the war.

"Looks empty," Royall said.

"Let's go on," Maddie said softly.

Mama gazed at the sky. "Could get rain tonight," she said. "Reckon we oughta take shelter in the house."

Maddie didn't want to set foot in the house, but she said nothing more as Royall stopped the wagon at the foot of the porch steps.

"That a garden over yonder?" Angeline asked.

"Weeds mostly," Mama said. "But maybe they left taters we can dig."

Pride jumped out of the wagon bed. He was halfway up the steps to the house when the front door opened and a gray-haired woman came out on the porch. Her skirts whispered as she moved toward them, reminding

Maddie of their former mistress in her silk gowns and soft kid slippers.

The woman withdrew a hand from the folds of her skirt, and it was then that Maddie saw the gun—a small gentleman's pistol, which flashed silver in the late afternoon sunlight.

"Don't come any closer," the woman said and pointed the pistol at them.

2

The gun was two feet from Pride's head. He stood perfectly still and didn't make a sound, but the soft brown eyes that sought out his mama were filled with fear.

Mama took a step toward him.

"Stay where you are!" the woman said sharply.

"I'm just comin' to get my boy," Mama said in an even voice. "Pride, come here to me."

Pride backed down one step. The barrel of the pistol shook a little and followed him.

"That's right," Mama said softly, her eyes fixed on the old woman and the gun. "Come to me."

Pride took another step and another. When he finally reached Mama, she pulled him to her in a brief hug and then stepped between him and the pistol.

"We didn't come to make trouble," she said to the woman. "Just lookin' to water the mules and find shelter for the night. We'll be goin' now."

Maddie and the others edged toward the wagon.

"Hold on!" the woman yelled to them.

They all turned to stare at her. Maddie noticed for the first time that the fabric of her gown was worn through in places, and her shoulders seemed to sag with weariness.

"Thought y'all were breakin' in on me," she said. "Can't be too careful these days."

"We just wanted a place to bed down," Mama said, still looking at the gun.

The woman looked hard at Mama, then at the rest of them. "Too many folks on the road with nothin' to lose—'cause they already lost it all." She saw Mama's eyes on the pistol and frowned. Finally, she lowered the gun.

Maddie saw Mama's shoulders drop and realized that Mama had been as scared as Maddie.

"Where you bound for?" the woman asked Mama. Her tone was still sharp, but she didn't seem nearly as frightening without the gun pointed at them.

"Wherever we can make a home," Mama said. "You got land you wanta sell?"

The woman's eyes narrowed. "Can't say as I do. Promised my husband I'd hold on—and I will as long as I can. You got money to pay for land?"

"Some," Mama said.

"How'd you get it?"

Mama pulled herself up straight and tall. "We come by it honest," Mama said.

The woman looked like she didn't believe that for a minute. "Makes you wonder what the world's comin' to—white folks losin' their land and slaves with money to buy it."

"Ain't no slaves no more," Zebedee said.

"Not around here, anyways." The woman's tone was bitter. "Most'a mine ran off when we got the news."

"How you gonna keep this place goin'?" Mama asked, and Maddie wondered why she cared. Why didn't she come on so they could get away from here?

The woman shook her head. "If my husband was here, he'd know."

"Where *is* your husband?"

"Killed in the Battle of Shiloh."

Mama's expression didn't change, but Maddie saw her lean a little toward the old white woman and knew that Mama was softening toward her. Losing a husband to the war was something Mama could understand.

"Mama," Maddie said. "We better be goin'. It'll be dark soon."

Miz Byrd looked at the sky, then back at Mama. "Help yourself to water," she said, not friendly, but not exactly mean either. "Well's back'a the house."

"Much obliged," Mama said.

"You can stay in one'a the cabins down the road if you've a mind to," the woman added. She turned to go back inside.

"We thank you," Mama called after her, but the old woman had already shut the door behind her.

Royall drove the wagon past the burned-out buildings. The trees thinned and they could see a row of slave cabins facing vast, unplowed fields.

Two young men and a girl about Maddie's age sat on tree stumps in front of one of the cabins. Nearby, a boy and girl of six or seven chased each other, laughing and hollering.

One of the men stood up when Royall stopped the wagon. He was tall, with broad shoulders and skin the color of ground coffee. He seemed friendly enough, but Maddie thought he looked watchful. She wondered if everybody in North Carolina was expecting trouble.

Royall jumped down from the wagon, and he and the tall man shook hands. The man's name was Daniel Parrish. He introduced the girl as his sister Ruth and the other man as Tom Spivey.

14

"Woman up at the Big House sez we can sleep here tonight," Royall said.

" 'Course you can." Ruth hurried over to the wagon, smiling at them. Maddie thought she was very pretty.

"You been travelin' all day?" Ruth asked. "Then you gotta be bone-tired. What a sweet baby," she said as Angeline climbed from the wagon with Elizabeth. "I'll help you carry your things to a cabin and you can have supper with us."

The two children had stopped running and were watching the new arrivals. Pride was staring back.

"Them's Tom's children," Ruth said to Pride. "George and Letty."

Mama's hand rested briefly on Pride's forehead. "Why don't you go play with 'em," she said, but Pride just sat in the wagon, looking shy.

"You come far?" Daniel asked Royall as he helped unhitch the mules.

"All the way from the coast," Royall said. "Roanoke Island. Y'all work on this plantation?"

"Daniel bought his freedom years ago, set up a leather shop over in Willoughby," Ruth said as she lifted bundles of bedding from the wagon. "He bought me my freedom 'fore the war started, and we's come back for our brother."

"Where's Willoughby?" Mama asked.

"Due west'a here," Daniel said. "Five or six days' ride by wagon."

"They sell land to coloreds over there?" Mama asked.

Daniel smiled. "Well, they sold me mine," he said.

This caught Zebedee's attention. "You got your own land? You got yourself a house?"

Daniel nodded.

15

"And you makes a livin' doin' leather work?"

"Ain't many shoes bein' bought since the war," Daniel said, "but soles and harnesses always need mendin'."

"Daniel's gonna teach our brother William the leather trade so's he can help," Ruth said as she headed for a cabin with a load of bundles.

Daniel led the mules to a trough of water. "Tom and his wife's goin' with us to Willoughby. You folks are welcome to come along."

"Might be safer than travelin' alone, Miz Ella," Royall said.

Mama nodded. She was watching Pride climb down from the wagon. When he started toward the two children, she smiled. "Much obliged," she said to Daniel. "When y'all leavin'?"

"Soon as I fix a wheel on my wagon," Daniel said. "May take a couple days."

Tom was laying kindling for a fire. A young woman with a baby on her hip came out of the cabin and walked over to stand with him.

"This here's my wife Reba," Tom said. "I reckon we ain't gonna miss this place when we goes."

"Amen," Reba said softly.

While the women cooked supper, Pride played a ring game with the Spivey children and the men sat talking.

"You work on a plantation on Roanoke Island?" Daniel asked Royall.

"Ain't no plantations on the island," Royall said. "The Union Army took it early in the war, and slaves come runnin' from all over to claim their freedom. That's what we done. Worked for the army buildin' a fort and docks."

"That so?" Daniel looked interested.

" 'Fore we went to the island, me and my children lived on a plantation owned by the McCarthas," Mama said. "Sometimes I ponder on how the war left 'em."

"You reckon they ever ponder on how the war left us?" Maddie asked.

Mama gave her a sharp look. "Mistress treated us better'n some," she said. "You always had a full belly and shoes on your feet, didn't you?"

Maddie's eyes dropped to her bare feet, now caked with mud. She saw Daniel looking at them, too. Suddenly it struck her that she must look a sight in her oldest homespun dress with mud splattered on the hem.

"Reckon so," Maddie muttered. "But there's things more important than shoes and a full belly. Leastways, Papa thought so."

"Where is your papa?" Ruth asked.

"Buried in Tennessee." Maddie glanced at Mama to see if the words had distressed her, but Mama was stirring a pot of greens and didn't look up. "Papa and Royall fought with the Union Army when they let colored men enlist," Maddie added. "Papa didn't come back."

"I'm sorry, Maddie," Ruth said softly.

"He must'a been a brave man," Daniel said. His voice was so kind Maddie felt her eyes sting. She blinked and looked away.

"Titus wuz the best man I ever knowed," Royall said. "We never woulda made it to Roanoke Island 'cept for him."

"You get that limp in the war?" Daniel asked Royall.

Royall nodded and rubbed his knee. "Minié ball near shot it to pieces."

"Reckon we owe you and Titus a debt," Daniel said.

17

Royall looked embarrassed. "Not me," he said. "I didn't do nothin' but stay alive."

There was silence for a moment. Then Ruth said, "Miz Ella, you wuz a house servant. You and Angeline and Maddie."

Mama nodded.

"How'd you know?" Angeline asked.

" 'Cause y'all talk like the mistress."

"House servants had it better," Tom said. "Ole Joseph never worked a day in the fields. Had him a fine suit'a clothes and all the master's whiskey he could drink."

"No slave had it better," Daniel said. "Like Maddie sez, clothes and such don't matter a tinker's damn."

Maddie looked up and their eyes met.

"What *does* matter to you, Miz Maddie?" Daniel asked. "Now the war's over and you got your freedom?"

The question startled Maddie. After living so long on the island among their friends, she wasn't used to strangers. And she sure wasn't used to strangers who asked whatever questions popped into their heads.

"I wanta see my family settled," Maddie said finally. "Then I'm goin' north."

"What you gonna do up North?"

"Go to school."

Zebedee tossed a stick into the fire and frowned. "Aw, Maddie, you done been to school on the island, plus helpin' Miz James teach us. You read better'n anybody. There's nothin' for you to learn up North."

"Always somethin' to learn," Maddie said. She had known that when the time came for her to leave, Zeb wouldn't be happy about it. Mama might understand,

18

but the others would find all kinds of reasons to keep her from going.

"You can read?" Ruth was beaming at Maddie. "Brother Isaac, our preacher back home, wants to bring in a teacher for the children. But you could teach 'em till then, couldn't you? And me, too. Could you teach me to read?"

"I 'spect I can," Maddie said.

Ruth hugged her and laughed. "Always did wanta know how to read. Now you'll just have to stay in Willoughby."

Ruth's happiness was contagious. Maddie found herself laughing along with the girl, and even Zebedee smiled.

They had just sat down to supper outside the Spiveys' cabin when Maddie saw two boys coming across the field.

"That's my brother William up ahead," Ruth said to Maddie. "He's two years younger'n me. The other one's his friend Ben."

Maddie noticed that Ruth wasn't smiling as her eyes watched the boys approach the cabins. In fact, she looked troubled.

"Lookee here, Will, we got company," the taller boy said when they reached the cabin yard. He was grinning, but Maddie saw no hint of welcome in the sharp eyes, which took them all in.

"You boys fill your plates," Ruth said.

"William, where you been?" Daniel asked. "You wuz s'posed to be helpin' me with the wagon wheel."

Looking sullen, William heaped corn cakes and greens on a tin plate.

19

"William, you hear me?"

"I heared," the boy muttered. He carried his plate to the other side of the cabin yard and sat down on a stump. Only then did he say, "Me'n Ben wuz fishin'."

"Where's the fish?"

William gave his brother an angry look. "Didn't catch none. Ain't my fault the fish wuzn't bitin'."

"Nobody said it was your fault," Ruth said quickly.

"Rim's bent on that wheel," Daniel said. "Gonna take some hard work to beat it out."

"Will and me's used to workin' hard," Ben said with a smirk. "We been slaves, you 'member. Slaves ain't good for much, but they knows how to work."

"Ben, let it be," Tom said.

"What you mean?" Ben asked in mock surprise. "You reckon I'm upsettin' the Big Man? I sho' wouldn't wanta do that. You hear that, Mister Daniel, sir? Didn't mean to hurt your feelins. No, sir."

William laughed. "Ben, he don't know about slaves. He ain't *been* here to see us work."

"Please don't," Ruth pleaded.

William hesitated; then he frowned. "You ain't been here neither, so don't be tellin' me what to do."

"Don't talk that way to your sister," Daniel said sharply.

"Man just can't stop givin' orders," William said to Ben. "Reckon you and me'll be givin' 'em now we's free?"

"Ain't gonna *take* none, that's for sure," Ben said. "I been beat and worked like a mule long's I can recollect. Don't plan on livin' like some'un's ole dog ever again."

"What *do* you plan on doin'?" Daniel asked him.

"Ben's comin' with us," William said quickly. He seemed to be daring Daniel to argue.

"That right?" Daniel asked Ben.

Ben's eyes narrowed as he studied Daniel's face. "Reckon I might just do that," he said finally. "Make me some money and then head on west. I hears they treats men like men out West—no matter their color."

"When Ben goes, I'm goin' with him," William said.

"But we just got back together," Ruth protested.

William scowled at her. "Bein' together didn't matter to you all them years."

Daniel stood up, looking like he might go after his brother. Ruth grabbed his arm, but he swept past her and yanked William to his feet.

"Time we had us a talk," Daniel said.

William glared at him but didn't resist when Daniel led him toward the fields.

Ruth's eyes were filled with tears.

"They'll work it out," Zebedee told her. "Folks get mad, but it don't mean nothin'."

Ruth smiled at Zebedee and wiped at her eyes.

Ben helped himself to a corn cake from Daniel's plate. "Shame to waste good vittles," he said, looking pleased with himself. "Reckon the Big Man won't mind."

3

After breakfast dishes were done, Mama said, "Now we got the chance, we best be doin' some washin'."

Today, Maddie was wearing her shoes and a clean dress, but she figured her traveling clothes could do with a wash. She and Zebedee got buckets and headed for the well.

"What you think about William?" Zebedee asked when they were away from the cabins.

"Don't rightly know what to think," Maddie said.

"Sho' wuz mean to his sister," Zebedee said. "And that Ben. You reckon it's a good idea to go off with 'em?"

"Daniel may help us find land to buy," Maddie said.

Zebedee didn't say anything, but Maddie could tell something was on his mind. "What you frettin' over?" she asked. "Don't you like Ruth and Daniel?"

"Ruth's got a good heart," Zebedee said. "Better'n William deserves."

"What about Daniel?"

"He's all right."

Maddie looked at Zeb, trying to read his face. Finally, she said, "Seems like a good man to me."

"I reckon," was all Zebedee would say.

They were coming back from the well when Maddie heard sounds in the woods, like twigs snapping and leaves rustling underfoot. She peered into the growth beside the trail, but she didn't see anything.

"You hear somethin'?" she asked Zebedee.

He listened. "Nothin' but the birds."

They walked on, but Maddie had the feeling they were being watched. She kept looking back over her shoulder.

"What's got into you?" Zebedee asked her. "There's nobody here but you and me."

Maddie was about to tell him he was probably right when she saw something move in the bushes.

"Who's there?" she called out.

"Maddie—" Zeb began.

"Hush," Maddie said.

She walked over to the bushes and parted them. A pale face stared up at her. Maddie was so startled, she jerked back. When she looked again, the face was gone. But even Zebedee heard the sounds of someone crashing through the undergrowth to get away.

"You seen who it wuz?" he asked.

"Not really," Maddie said. She had seen the face for only a moment, a small face framed with wild yellow hair. A child. A little girl, she thought. But what would a little white girl be doing in these woods?

Maddie meant to ask someone if they'd seen a white child on the plantation, but when she and Zebedee got back, Mama had her heating the water, sweeping the cabin, and helping with the wash. Before she knew it, the morning was gone and Maddie had forgotten all about the child.

For supper, Mama served up a pot of stew and bread she had baked on the coals.

"Ruth spent all mornin' diggin' taters for the stew," Mama said.

"And come back with two," Ruth said, laughing at herself.

"Two's plenty to give it taste," Mama assured her.

Maddie was glad to see that Ben and William were silent tonight. They filled their plates and moved away to eat.

Reba fixed her children's plates and her own. Then she heaped food on a fourth plate. Maddie watched her carry it to the edge of the woods, set it on a flat stone, and come back to her own supper.

What a peculiar thing to do, Maddie was thinking, when she saw a small figure emerge from the trees, grab the plate, and dart back into the thicket. It happened so fast, Maddie was left with only a vague impression of a scrawny child in a gray shift—a child with crinkly yellow hair that sprang out in all directions.

"Who was that?" Maddie wasn't aware that she had interrupted Angeline or that everybody was staring at her. "Reba, what's a white child doin' here?"

"Ain't no white child," Reba said. She broke a hunk of bread in two and placed the pieces on George and Letty's plates. "That be Dessie's girl."

"Who's Dessie?" Maddie asked.

"One'a Master Byrd's slaves. Worked in the kitchen." Reba gazed into the woods where the child had disappeared. "Poor little thing. Ain't been right since the soldiers come."

"It wuz two summers ago," Tom said. "Them horses come thunderin' in and stomped the corn and 'bacco plants right into the ground. Then the soldiers set a torch to the outbuildin's. Ain't never seen such a

24

burnin'. Flames wuz fillin' the sky and lickin' at the clouds."

"The child—Dessie's girl," Maddie said. "Where was she when the soldiers came?"

"In the kitchen yard," Reba said. "Tibby—that be her name—weren't much more'n a knee baby then. Used to play 'round the yard with the chicks and watch for her mama."

"I wuz bringin' the mules in from the fields when the soldiers come stormin' into the kitchen yard," Tom said. "And there wuz Tibby—them horses rearin' and stompin' all around her. But somehow she got away and I seen her go into the barn—right 'fore they torched it."

"Lord'a mercy," Mama whispered.

"Then I seen Dessie runnin' for the barn," Tom went on. "That ole barn wuz lit up like sunrise, but Dessie went in anyhow. I followed her, but the smoke wuz so thick I couldn't see nothin'. Couldn't hardly breathe, neither."

Tom wiped his face on his sleeve, looking shaken. "I backed out into the air and then Dessie come out carryin' the girl," he said. "Dessie's skirt wuz on fire, so I took the child and set her down and tried to beat out the flames. Dessie wuz screamin' somethin' awful—it wuz like nothin' human I ever heared."

"She died next day," Reba said.

"What happened to Tibby?" Maddie asked softly.

"Run off into the woods," Reba said. "Tom and me found her curled up under a log. Didn't cry nor speak, just lay there starin' at nothin'. We took her back to the cabin with us."

"But ever' time we turned our backs, she run off,"

Tom added. "We'd go get her, bring her back, she'd run off again. Atter a while, we just let her be."

"We sets out food for her," Reba said, "and when it's cold, she slips in the cabin and sleeps by the door. But soon as she sees us awake, she's off like a rabbit."

"The child's outta her head," Tom said. "Ain't said a word since the burnin'."

"That who you saw in the woods this mornin'?" Zebedee asked Maddie.

Maddie nodded. "But I thought she was a white child. Reba, she surely looks white."

Reba and Tom exchanged uneasy looks.

"What?" Maddie frowned, watching them. "What is it you're not tellin'?"

"There wuz talk in the cabins, that's all," Reba said in a low voice. "Some said Tibby was Master's child, but Dessie never let on."

"The devil's spawn, more like it." Ben was standing over them, so close that Maddie could feel his warm breath on her face. He was scowling and his eyes looked too bright, like Pride's when he had the fever. "That child's no good to nobody," Ben said. "Be better if she'd burned with Dessie."

"Don't say that!" Mama admonished him. "*Whoever* sired her, the child's not to blame."

"Don't matter," Ben said harshly. "The whites don't want her, and the coloreds be fools to take her in."

Later, Maddie sat alone by the fire. The picture of a little girl in the midst of flames and rearing horses was fixed in her head, and she couldn't get rid of it.

Zebedee came and sat down beside her.

"She couldn't be more'n six," Maddie said, taking it

26

for granted that Zebedee would know she was thinking about Tibby. "How can she take care of herself?"

"Reba gives her food," Zebedee said. "Maybe she don't need much more'n that."

"She needs lots more." Suddenly Maddie turned to Zebedee, looking troubled. "I never knew what it was like out here," she said. "While we were on the island, all this was happenin' and I didn't know. Papa took us to the island to be safe. I wish we'd never come back."

"Titus took you to the island so's you could be *free*," Zebedee said. "I 'spect bein' free ain't the safest way to live."

Maddie frowned. Zeb was right, of course. Papa hadn't been thinking about safety when he took them to the island. They would have been safer on the plantation than running for their freedom. But Papa had believed freedom was worth any risk. Only now that she had seen the risks up close, Maddie wasn't so sure.

"What's gonna happen to Tibby when Reba and Tom leave?" Maddie wondered aloud.

Zebedee shook his head. He didn't have an answer. Finally he said, "I knows how it pains you to see a child in need, but you can't do for ever'body. No tellin' how many children's been left alone and hungry on account'a the war, and you can't help 'em all. But, Maddie,"—he hesitated, not sure how to say what he was thinking—"if you had babies of your own, you could see they wuz fed and loved and kept safe. I been studyin' on it, Maddie Henry, and I thinks it's time you settled down."

Maddie hadn't been expecting this, and she didn't want to think about what his words might mean. "Zeb—"

"Listen, I know you wants to go north and see all

27

them places Miz James talked about," he said in a rush, "but there's folks here that cares about you and don't want you to go. Ain't makin' a home for the folks you love about the best thing you can do with your freedom?"

The firelight danced across Zebedee's face. He looked shy and earnest. And so filled with hope that it hurt Maddie to see it.

Dear Zeb. She longed to throw her arms around him and tell him—what? That she loved him like a brother? But that wouldn't do. For Zebedee, Maddie realized now, that wouldn't be nearly enough.

"You don't have to say nothin'," Zebedee said. His voice sounded weary. "Just somethin' I been thinkin' on, but it don't matter."

Later, lying on her pallet beside the open cabin door, too many thoughts and people filled Maddie's head. Zeb. Tibby. Papa. Mama. Miz James. They all crowded in, their faces floating under her closed lids until they made her dizzy.

Maddie sat up and peered through the door at the sky, but there were no stars tonight. Then she noticed someone sitting by the fire. His face was in darkness, but the firelight caught and flickered on the barrel of his rifle. She wondered what he was doing alone in the dark, and then it came to her: While the rest of them slept, Daniel was watching and listening, making sure no harm came to them.

Maddie lay back down and closed her eyes. Her family's soft, steady breathing soon lulled her to sleep.

4

Daniel was striking the bent wheel rim with a hammer. The clang of iron hitting iron echoed across the cabins and fields. Zebedee was sanding the broken wheel, and Tom and Royall were carving new spokes. William sat with them, making lethargic swipes at a stick of wood with his knife.

"Reckon that wheel can be mended?" Angeline asked as she stitched up a tear in one of Royall's shirts.

"Daniel can fix anything," Ruth said.

The women sat in the shade at the edge of the woods. Mama, Angeline, and Reba sewed while Maddie and Ruth played with Elizabeth and Reba's baby, Nathan.

The babies were lying on a quilt spread on the grass. Ruth tickled their feet with a dried cornshuck and sang to them.

> *Ole black bull come down the hollow,*
> *Shake his tail, you hear him bellow.*
> *When he bellow, he jar the river,*
> *He paw the earth, he make it quiver.*
> *Who-zen-John, who-za.*

Angeline looked up from the mending, her eyes soft as they rested on Ruth and the babies. "You got a way with 'em," she said.

Ruth's face glowed as she watched the babies kick their feet and grab for the cornshuck. "I'm gonna have lots'a babies," she said. "Lots and lots'a babies."

Maddie watched Ruth pick up Nathan and cradle him in her arms. She had that look—at once tender and strong—that Mama used to get when Pride was a lap baby, the same look Angeline had when she cuddled Elizabeth. They knew—Mama, Angeline, and Ruth—that motherhood would bring them their greatest joy, despite the fears and troubles that came with it.

Maddie envied them their fierce certainty. She touched Elizabeth's plump hand, and the baby's smile yanked at her heart. It would be so easy to follow Mama and Angeline's path, to forget the dreams Miz James had awakened in her. And how hard it would be to leave them all! Mama and Angeline. Pride. Royall. Elizabeth. And Zeb. Especially Zeb.

In her mind, Maddie saw that grin of his and heard him say, "What you think'a that, Maddie Henry?" He used her full name, he said, because it was a fine thing to have two names now that slave times were over.

How hard it would be to leave.

And yet, Maddie knew she would go—just as surely as Papa had known that one day they would run for freedom. "You're two of a kind," Mama had always said. "Can't decide who's most stubborn, you or your papa." Dreamers, she had called them, with affection and fear in her voice. And sometimes anger as well. But she must have always known that she wouldn't be able to hold them back.

When supper was ready, Reba fixed Tibby's plate and set it near the woods. But this time, when the girl came out to get her food, Ben ran up behind her and blocked her retreat.

Tibby froze, terror gleaming in her eyes. She darted to the left, but Ben jumped in front of her. She veered to the right, and he blocked her way again.

"Ben, let that girl be!" Tom shouted.

But Ben ignored him, grinning and lunging as though he meant to grab her.

The child shrank back, but there was nowhere to go. Ben was in front of her, a circle of strangers behind her. Never had Maddie seen such panic and torment in a child's face.

In a rush of pity and fury, Maddie ran to Tibby and gripped the girl's shoulders. Tibby shrieked in alarm and stiffened under Maddie's hands, but Ben's grinning face kept her from pulling away.

"It's all right, Tibby," Maddie said softly. But she was looking at Ben and her eyes blazed. "Nobody's gonna hurt you."

Ben was smirking and dancing around them. He moved closer and Tibby pressed herself into Maddie's side.

"Get away from this child," Maddie said, still not raising her voice. "You so much as touch her, I'll claw your eyes out."

Ben laughed, but before he could take another step toward them, Tom and Daniel were there. They grabbed Ben's arms and jerked them back. Ben struggled to free himself, grunting and cursing.

"You pull too hard, I'll break your shoulder," Daniel said.

Maddie sank to the ground and took Tibby into her arms. The sour odor of unwashed flesh was strong.

31

Maddie stroked the girl's hair, feeling twigs and burrs matted in its tangles. But before Maddie could speak to her, Tibby slipped from Maddie's arms and bolted for the woods. Her supper plate lay overturned in the dirt.

Daniel and Tom had marched Ben out behind the cabins for a talking-to. While she washed the supper dishes, Maddie heard Daniel's voice—she couldn't make out the words, but it was clear enough that he was giving Ben a piece of his mind. Sometimes Ben butted in, protesting, but Daniel cut him off. William was listening, too. He sat by the fire, frowning, shoulders hunched. Whenever Daniel's voice rose, William would glance that way, his frown deepening.

William's silent anger troubled Maddie. He put her in mind of an old hunting dog back on the plantation. When the dog turned snappish and strange one day, they'd tied him up in the kitchen yard. He just sat there giving them mean looks, but quiet, like he wouldn't hurt a fly—until somebody came close to him. Then he'd leap to his feet and charge at them, snarling, teeth bared, baying his fury to the skies. Folks learned to give that old dog his space.

When the dishes were done, Maddie filled a plate with food and carried it to the woods. She set it down and went back to the cabin, but every now and then she'd look out to see if Tibby had come for her food. The evening passed, darkness gathered, and the plate was still there.

Maddie stood at the door of the cabin as everyone was settling down for the night. She was still hoping to see Tibby dash out of the woods and claim her supper.

"She won't come now."

Daniel had appeared from around the corner of

32

the cabin. He lowered his rifle and leaned against the doorframe.

"Reckon she's too scared," Maddie said.

"She'll be out later, after ever'body's asleep."

The look Maddie gave him was curious. "How do you know?"

" 'Cause she comes to the cabins ever' night," Daniel said. "I stay in the shadows and watch her."

"Watch her do what?"

"If you stay awake, you'll see for yourself," he said.

With that, Daniel touched the brim of his hat and went on with his rounds.

Maddie settled down on her quilt beside the door and waited. The stars came out and grew bright in the sky. Sometimes she would see Daniel walking around the cabin area or stoking the fire to warm up coffee from supper. It seemed that hours had passed, and Maddie was growing tired and sleepy.

Elizabeth whimpered and Maddie heard rustling as Angeline moved to comfort her. Maddie stretched out her cramped legs and yawned. It was foolish to lose sleep waiting for something that might never happen. But she continued to wait and was finally rewarded.

Daniel had just gone to the back of the cabins when a small, familiar figure stepped from the dark woods, hesitated, then came slowly toward the fire. Maddie shrank back into the darkness of the cabin, hardly daring to breathe lest Tibby see her and run away.

The child surveyed the cabin yard as she approached the fire. Then she stood completely still, listening. Maddie listened, also—to the croaking of frogs on the river and the whisper of leaves stirred by a gentle breeze. After a moment, Tibby appeared satisfied and moved on. Maddie watched as the child walked slowly around the fire, her pale face luminous in the fire-light. Gradually, Tibby began to sway as she walked, to lift her arms, and dip her body rhythmically. Maddie was startled, then amazed, when she realized that the girl was dancing.

Tibby's movements were surprisingly graceful as she circled the fire. Her feet began to move faster. She pranced and whirled beside the flames. And then she stopped.

Maddie expected the girl to dart away, but Tibby raised one hand in a willowy sweep and sank into a deep bow. That was when Maddie realized that Tibby was watching—and dancing with—her own shadow. Tibby drew herself up tall and the shadow lengthened. She stooped low and the shadow shrank. She circled the shadow and it followed her, seeming to spring and frolic on its own. At times, Tibby would reach out her arms, as though drawing the shadow to her, and then she would release it and go on with her dance. Maddie couldn't see Tibby's features in the dim light, but she could tell from the girl's movements that—for this moment, at least—she was happy and unafraid.

Tibby stopped dancing again, but this time she looked anxiously toward the cabins. She stared into the darkness for an instant, and then she ran. In a moment, she had disappeared into the trees.

Wide awake now, Maddie wondered at what she had just witnessed. This wild, terrified child could dance more gracefully and joyfully than anyone she had ever seen. Where had she learned to do it? And what did it mean? When Daniel came back to sit by the fire, Maddie joined him.

Daniel listened as Maddie told him about seeing Tibby dance with her shadow. "Tom sez she's been doin' it a long time," he said.

Maddie gazed into the flames. "You'd think she'd be afraid of fire after what happened to her mama."

"Reckon she knows the difference 'tween a friendly fire and a hurtful one," Daniel said.

"Why you think she does it?"

He shook his head. "The old slaves used to say that shadows wuz the spirits of loved ones come back from the grave. Could be the girl thinks it's her mama come back."

"Or she just figgers shadows are kinder than people," Maddie said.

Daniel nodded. "Couldn't rightly argue that one with her," he said.

5

Next morning, Royall and Daniel put the mended wheel on the wagon.

Royall stood back and looked at it. "Good as new."

"Reckon we can move out in the mornin'," Daniel said.

Mama and Angeline went to Reba's cabin to help her pack up, while Maddie swept out the wagon bed. Ruth and Zebedee started carrying Reba and Tom's belongings to be loaded on the wagon.

"You like livin' in Willoughby?" Maddie asked Ruth.

Ruth set a heavy cooking pot into the wagon and stopped to catch her breath. "It's a good place," she said. "Folks don't bother us none—leastways, most of 'em don't."

"Not all?"

"There's a few don't want coloreds livin' in their town," Ruth said. "Like Owen Gentry—he runs the general store and most ever'thing else. Best to stay outta his way."

Daniel was sitting nearby cleaning the mules' harnesses. "Whites and coloreds don't mix much in Willoughby."

"But ever'body brings their shoes and bridles to Daniel, colored and white," Ruth said.

"Too much work for one man," Daniel said. "How'd

you like to help me out, Zebedee? Couldn't pay much, but I'd teach you leather work."

Zebedee didn't respond at once and Maddie just stared at him, wondering why he wasn't jumping at a chance to make some money and learn a trade. "Sounds like a right good offer," she said.

Looking thoughtful, Zebedee nodded. "It does, and I thank you," he said to Daniel. "Only the Henrys may be needin' me to plow and plant."

"We could work it so you'd have time for both," Daniel said.

Zebedee nodded again. "Thought you wuz gonna teach William the leather trade," he said.

"I am," Daniel said, "but it's no harder to teach two. And I reckon William needs him some time just to be free."

Ruth looked surprised; then she smiled at her brother.

"I'd have work to keep the both'a you busy a few days a week," Daniel went on. "It's up to you, Zeb."

Zebedee looked at Maddie, then back at Daniel. "It's a fine offer, and I accept," he said. "That is, if we find land to buy in Willoughby."

"I'll take y'all out to see the feller that sold me mine," Daniel said.

"I been thinkin' on how lucky we is," Ruth said. "On the trip over here, we seen so many poor folks on the road with nowheres to go. Some didn't have nothin' but the shirts on their backs."

William had just walked up. He leaned against the wagon, chewing on a piece of broom straw. "Least they ain't slaves no more," he said.

"Neither are you," Ruth said softly. "Time to leave them days behind."

37

"Reckon that's easy for you," he muttered. "Feel'a the whip ain't so fresh on your back." He threw the broom straw down and walked off.

Maddie and Zebedee got busy loading a cornshuck mattress into the wagon, acting as though they hadn't heard anything.

"He weren't always like this," Ruth said. "William wuz the sweetest little boy. Used to run up to me and hug me so hard I'd lose my breath. You 'member, Daniel?"

Daniel nodded.

Ruth looked at Maddie and Zebedee. "Daniel wuz the shoemaker here," she said. "Master Byrd let him hire out to the other plantations after his own work wuz done. He saved ever' cent till he had enough to buy his freedom. Told William and me he'd save up and buy ours, too. But the way William saw it, Daniel walked out on him."

Daniel kept cleaning the strip of leather in his hand, but Maddie saw his mouth tighten and knew that Ruth's words were causing him pain.

"Daniel bought his shop and saved more money," Ruth went on. " 'Fore the war started, he come for me. Daniel told William he'd be back for him, but William didn't believe it. All he knew wuz Daniel had left him; now I wuz goin'. He done lit into me, kickin' and screamin'. Said he'd hate me till the day he died." Ruth's voice shook a little. "I never shoulda gone."

"You had to go!" Daniel said sharply. "Old man Byrd wuz after you the same way he pestered Dessie. I didn't wanta leave William here any more'n you did, but you had to get away."

"Don't matter," Ruth said. "I never shoulda left without him."

Maddie put her arm around Ruth's shoulders.

"How come Mister Byrd wuz willin' to let you and Ruth go?" Zebedee asked Daniel.

"Needed the money," Daniel said. "This place wuz goin' down even 'fore the war. He wuz sellin' off slaves and parcels'a land ever-which-a-way."

"William don't even wanta be around me," Ruth said. "Only one he'll talk to is Ben."

Daniel grunted. "Can't figger out what William sees in that boy."

"He needed *somebody*," Ruth said.

"After him scarin' that little girl, I don't know if I want Ben comin' to Willoughby," Daniel said.

"He's a free man," Ruth pointed out. "He can go anywhere he wants."

"But he don't have to go there with me!"

"If you say Ben can't come, William won't either," Ruth said. "I want that sweet boy back," she added softly. "Daniel, can't you at least try?"

"I been tryin'," Daniel said. But the look on his face told Maddie that Ben would be going with them to Willoughby.

When her chores were done that afternoon, Maddie took Pride and Reba's children to the fields to pick wild strawberries.

"If we get enough, we'll have strawberries with breakfast all the way to Willoughby," Maddie told them. But since the children were eating more berries than they dropped in their buckets, Maddie figured they'd be lucky to have enough for one breakfast.

Pride seemed happier than Maddie had seen him in a long time as he hopped from vine to vine, chattering with George and Letty and exclaiming over the berries

39

he found. Mama had always thought they were better than the field workers, so back on the plantation, she hadn't let Pride mix with the children on slave row. Then, on the island, Pride had been too sick to play with the other children. This was the first chance he'd had to make friends his own age.

"There's lots'a berries over here!" George called out.

"Don't take 'em all," Letty warned her brother.

"There's plenty, Letty," Pride assured the girl. He dropped a handful of berries into Letty's bucket. She beamed at him.

When her bucket was nearly filled, Maddie sat down to wait for the children. Their shrieks and laughter filled the warm afternoon air and mixed with the voices from the cabins, where wagons were being loaded and supper begun.

Maddie felt a twinge of excitement as she thought about setting out for Willoughby. In a few days, her family would see the town that could become their home—the first home that would really belong to them.

On the island, the army had given each family an acre of land. Maddie's family had built themselves a log house and planted a garden. Maddie remembered how happy they'd been the day the house was finished. Then, near the end of the war, the government decided to give the land back to the white men who had owned it before the fighting started. Most of the Henrys' friends refused to leave the homes they had built, but Mama figured there was no good purpose in trying to fight the whole United States government. So they left Roanoke Island. They left their house and their friends. And sometimes, Maddie felt they had left Papa, too.

Maddie forced herself back from those painful days

and studied the land around her. Fields of rich, dark earth where corn would grow tall and sturdy. Pastures so green that cattle could eat their fill for a year and still come back for more. But there was no corn. There were no cattle. Just the land, lying still and useless and bathed in yellow light.

The girl appeared while Maddie waited. She came to the edge of a stand of bald cypress trees and stopped, watching Maddie. When Maddie's eyes came to rest on her, Tibby moved back a half step, but she didn't run.

Afraid that any movement might startle her, Maddie sat very still. They stayed that way a long time, just looking at one another, until Pride and the Spivey children came whooping and hollering to show Maddie their harvest.

Next morning, Maddie made a nest of quilts in their wagon, where Angeline, Elizabeth, and Pride would ride. The men were hitching up the mules, while the women packed up the last of their belongings and shooed the excited children out of their way.

When Mama brought out a bundle of food to put in the wagon, Maddie said, "We can't leave the girl to fend for herself. I wanta take her."

Mama found a space for the food in the wagon bed. "You seen her this mornin'?" she asked.

"No'm."

"Then how you gonna find her?"

"She's close by," Maddie said. "She watches ever'thing we do."

Mama turned around to look at Maddie. "You figger she'll let you load her in the wagon like a sack'a meal? That girl's wild, Maddie."

"I know. But we can't leave her."

Reba came over carrying Nathan. "I feels bad about goin' without her, too," she said to Maddie, "but I don't hardly see what else we can do."

Maddie's eyes darted across the trees where Tibby came to get her food. She had been thinking about the child all night, worrying about how Tibby would get by without Reba and Tom. Reba patted Maddie's arm. "She'll start bird-dogging the Big House once we's gone. Mistress won't let her starve."

Picturing that bitter woman with her pistol brought Maddie little comfort. "I'm goin' to look for her," she said.

"And do what if you find her?" Mama demanded. "Throw her down and rope her like a calf? Maddie, that child can't be drug off against her will. That's what this freedom is—no more forcin' folks to go where they don't wanta go. Even if Miz Maddie thinks it's the right thing for 'em."

"Mama, you know it's not like that." Maddie's eyes pleaded with her mama to understand.

Mama's face softened. "I know it's hard," she said, "But this ain't the first hard thing you've had to do, and it won't be the last."

When the wagons pulled out from the cabins, Maddie trailed behind. Her eyes searched the woods and fields for Tibby. Maddie called her name, over and over, but there was no response. When the wagons passed through the open gate, and Maddie could no longer see the plantation house through the trees, she knew there was nothing more she could do.

Zebedee and Ruth came to walk with her. Neither of

42

them said anything, but it was a comfort to Maddie to have them there.

Daniel took a road that would lead to a bridge where they could cross the river. Royall followed in the second wagon.

Maddie felt a hard knot in her chest, which seemed to grow with each step she took. More than once, she came close to running back to the plantation to look for Tibby. But she knew that her place was with her family.

They stayed on the narrow, rutted road until they came to the bridge. Maddie was gazing across the water to the opposite shore when Zebedee touched her arm and pointed behind them.

Maddie looked back, and way down the road, she could see someone coming toward them. Her heart lurched and she glanced at Zebedee. He was smiling.

Maddie looked at the road again. The lone traveler was still coming, her wild yellow hair glowing in the morning sun.

6

It was a good, flat road that led into Willoughby, made of packed dirt and wide enough for two wagons to pass easily. But the buildings that lined either side of the road had seen better days. Signs on the storefronts were faded, and paint peeled from the walls.

As they came into town, Maddie saw an old colored man pushing a cart filled with strawberries. "Berries, fresh strawberries!" he called to them. "Ten cents silver—thirty dollars Confederate money. Fresh strawberries!"

Ruth waved to him and he waved back.

"That's Old Josh," she said to Maddie and Zebedee. "Him and his boys is sharecroppin' now they're free."

Since Maddie had spent her whole life on an isolated plantation, and then on the island, she was excited about seeing a town—even a small one like Willoughby. She craned her neck, trying to take in everything at once: the man at the smithy shoeing a skinny horse, the ladies in bonnets gathered on the wooden sidewalks to talk, the man with an empty sleeve carrying a sack of flour to his wagon. Except for Old Josh, all the faces were white.

The blacksmith raised his hand when Daniel drove by, but the rest offered nothing more than curious stares as the wagons creaked past. Maddie felt uneasy being looked at up and down by all these people. She glanced at Zebedee and saw that he gazed straight ahead as he walked, his eyes fixed on the back of Royall's wagon.

Maddie looked back for Tibby and didn't see her. But after watching the child follow them for nearly a week, Maddie had no doubt that Tibby was somewhere close by. Being fearful of people, she'd most likely stay clear of the road as long as they were in town.

They passed a building that had a fresh coat of white paint and a fancy sign with black-and-gold lettering, which read *General Store*. Two men were leaning on the hitching post out front. One of them had a thatch of gray hair and was wearing a white apron. He stopped talking when he saw the wagons and turned around to get a good look. Maddie saw him shake his head, say something to the other man, and spit into the dirt.

"That's Owen Gentry," Ruth said in a low voice. "Reckon he's not happy to see more coloreds comin' to town. The other one's Walter Newsome, and he's near as bad."

Maddie felt the men's eyes boring into her back as the wagons moved slowly out of town.

Suddenly Ruth exclaimed, "There's our place!" and pointed to a little house of weathered gray wood set back from the road.

Daniel pulled into the packed-earth yard and stopped his wagon in front of the house. Royall did the same.

Bright flowers bloomed around the steps of the house. A smaller building stood nearby—Daniel's leather shop, Maddie figured—and there was a garden behind the house.

While everyone was getting out of the wagons, Maddie looked back down the road. She could see the town from here, and folks going about their business, but there was still no sign of Tibby. Maddie was beginning to worry. What if the sight of all those people had made Tibby run off? What if she was lost out there, alone and far away from anything she knew? But then Maddie saw the yellow head bobbing in an overgrown field this side of town.

Relief washed over her as she watched the girl make her way slowly through the tall weeds. How strange this place must seem to her, Maddie thought. And how tired she must be after walking so far. If this journey to an unknown town was frightening for Maddie, how much more frightening it must be for Tibby—who didn't even know where she was going.

Maddie waited until she was sure that Tibby had seen her. Then she waved. Tibby stopped, standing very still for a moment. Then she raised a hand briefly in reply.

Daniel and Ruth's house was too small to hold them all, so they sat outside and ate cold sweet potatoes and corn cakes. When Maddie left Tibby's plate at the edge of the field, the child grabbed it and withdrew into the weeds.

"Miz Ella, a man name'a Judd Loftis sold me my land," Daniel said. "I'll take y'all to see him after dinner."

"Mister Loftis givin' shares to folks that wants to work his land," Tom said. "If he's a mind to give me and Ruth a share, Daniel sez we can keep half the profits."

"You trust a white man to let you keep anything?" Ben demanded.

"I've knowed Mister Loftis a long time," Daniel said. "He's a man'a his word."

Ben just smirked and shook his head.

Out the road from Daniel and Ruth's place, they passed a big white house that put Maddie in mind of her old plantation home. A few cows grazed in the pasture, but the fields lay fallow.

"That's Mister Gentry's place," Ruth said. "Used to have more cows and horses than you could shake a stick at, but the army took most of 'em."

They came to a field of new corn, which stretched from the road to the horizon. Men, women, and children moved slowly down the rows plucking out weeds with their grub hoes. In the next field, folks were digging up potatoes.

"All them folks works for Mister Loftis," Ruth said. "Gentry land's just settin' there 'cause he ain't about to share his crops with coloreds, but Mister Loftis—he knows times is changed."

A string of cabins stood at the edge of the potato field. Old women sat outside watching little children run and play in the dirt. Maddie gazed at the cabins, thinking about slave row back on the McCartha plantation.

Ruth's eyes followed Maddie's. "That's where the workers and their families live."

"Not much different from slave times," Maddie said.

" 'Ceptin' now they gets to sell part'a the crops they raise," Ruth said. "Ever'body sez Mister Loftis be a fair man."

"He owned slaves," Maddie said.

47

"But he wuzn't like the Gentrys and the Newsomes," Ruth said. "I never heared'a Mister Loftis whuppin' or sellin' nobody."

Maddie didn't say anything, but she was thinking how her people had always been thankful for the small kindnesses in their lives. How Mama was still grateful to Mistress for giving them shoes and teaching her to read. Back on the plantation, when somebody spoke ill of the master or mistress, Mama would say, "Least I got a roof over my head and I know my babies won't be sold right outta my arms." But those few blessings didn't make keeping slaves any less wrong, Maddie thought.

The Loftis house wasn't nearly so fine as Owen Gentry's. It was just a big, square farmhouse with a porch across the front. Daniel pulled the wagon to a stop in the kitchen yard, where a white man was nailing wire to a chicken coop. When the man saw Daniel, he came over to the wagons.

Maddie was surprised when Daniel called him Mister Loftis because he didn't look like any plantation owner she had ever seen. His shirt was patched and he had the leathery face of someone who was used to working in the sun. She was even more surprised to see the man reach for Daniel's outstretched hand and shake it.

"Tom and Reba here's lookin' for land to work," Daniel said. "Told 'em you might be able to help 'em, Mister Loftis. They's good workers."

"I reckon we can do somethin'," Mister Loftis said to Tom, "seein' as how Daniel's vouchin' for you."

Reba and Tom grinned at each other. While Mister Loftis talked to them, Maddie looked around. She noticed a tall white boy with rusty-colored hair sitting on the back porch watching them. When he saw Maddie looking, he smiled. Startled, Maddie dropped her eyes. She couldn't remember white folks ever smiling at her—except for Miz James and Sergeant Taylor back on the island, and they were different from anybody she'd ever known.

"My boy'll take you to your cabin," Mister Loftis was saying to Tom. "Sam!" he called to the boy on the porch. "Take these folks to the cabins. And show 'em the field 'cross the creek. Tell Jack to get 'em the tools they need."

The boy loped over and climbed into the wagon with Reba, Tom, and their children. Tom took the reins and they started back down the road.

Mister Loftis turned to Royall. "You lookin' for land to work?"

"No, sir. We's lookin' for land to buy," Royall said. "Hope to find us a nice little farm."

The man looked thoughtful. Then he said to Daniel, "You know the Finley place out the road? I bought it when the old man died. Ain't done nothin' with it and I reckon I won't now."

Daniel nodded. "Nice piece'a land," he said.

"Near fifty acres," Mister Loftis said to Royall. "But it ain't been worked in years. Gonna take some coaxin' to bring it back."

Royall grinned. "Don't mind coaxin', Mister Loftis." Then his grin faded. "Iffen the price ain't too high."

"I reckon you got Confederate dollars."

"No, sir," Royall said. "We got silver."

"Well, then," Mister Loftis said, looking pleased. "Let's drive out there and look the place over."

The house stood in the middle of an open field. Faded silver-gray by years of rain and sun, it squatted in the shade of old oak and sweet gum trees. Behind the house was a barn, which leaned and had planks missing; a little pond; and a cluster of neglected apple trees.

When the wagon stopped in front of the house, Maddie held back, not joining the others. Her eyes moved over every inch of the house and barn, then on to the fields. Fences were down and holes gaped in the roof of the barn. Tall weeds and grass nearly hid the porch from view. But none of that mattered to Maddie—because *this* was what Papa had always dreamed of for them. A real house with a front porch. Fields just waiting to be plowed and planted. Trees for his children and grandchildren to climb and a pasture where his animals could graze.

Royall and Zebedee were following Mister Loftis to the barn, with William and Ben trailing behind. Pride raced through the tall grass to the pond. And Mama and Angeline stood on the porch.

"Maddie, come on!" Mama called, and Maddie tore off for the house.

It was cool and dimly lit inside, smelling of dust and dampness. There was a front room with a smoke-blackened fireplace, a small room at the back, and a lean-to storeroom. A ladder in the front room led to the sleeping loft. The worn, heart-pine floor felt silky-smooth under Maddie's bare feet, and the windows had glass in them.

Maddie studied the window in the front room, too dirty now to see through, and thought about the day they'd finished the log house on the island. Papa had been so proud of that house, and he'd promised Mama that one day she'd have a plank floor and real glass in the windows. Maddie could still see him smiling when

50

Mama said, "Glass windows couldn't make me any happier than I am this minute."

Royall came running into the house. "He'll sell it to us, Miz Ella," Royall said. "Iffen you wants it. And he sez we can buy a cow from him. What you think, Miz Ella?"

Mama was gazing at the glass window. She put an arm around Maddie's waist, another around Angeline's, and she said, "What I think is—we've found ourselves a home."

7

Mama and Angeline were sweeping out dirt and leaves from the house, while Maddie and the men unloaded their belongings from the wagon. Mama came out to the porch, broom in hand, and surveyed the piles of bedding and cooking pots at the foot of the steps.

"Angeline's scrubbin' the storeroom so we can put food and dishes away," Mama said. She handed her broom to Maddie. "Sweep the porch and we'll pile up ever'thing out here till we get the house ready."

"Chimney's full'a leaves and birds' nests," Royall said. "Till I clean it, you best be cookin' outside, Miz Ella."

Angeline came out to the porch. The front of her dress was wet, and she was picking bits of cobweb from her hair. "This place is a mess," she said. "When I tried to climb the ladder to the loft, it broke."

"Pride can sleep in the back room with me till we get the ladder fixed," Mama said. "The rest'a you'll have to make do with the front room."

"Zeb and me can sleep on the porch," Maddie said.

"I 'spect you and Royall's plannin' on buildin' your own house," Mama said to Angeline.

"Once we get this place fixed up," Angeline said. "I

was thinkin' the hill beyond the pond might be a good spot, if it's all right with you, Mama."

"This land belongs to all of us," Mama said. "You and Royall build wherever you like."

"Don't that sound good?" Zebedee was looking out over the fields and grinning. "We's legal landowners now—not just squatters."

"Now that we's landowners, we gotta think about puttin' in crops," Royall said.

"It's late to be plantin'," Mama said.

"There's still time to put in vegetables to see us through the winter," Royall said. "And I reckon we better plant some corn—enough for us and some to sell."

"We got enough to buy seed?" Mama asked.

"*Just* enough," Royall said, "after we pay Mister Loftis for the cow."

"Zeb'll be workin' for Daniel and bringin' in a little money," Maddie said. Zeb nodded, but Maddie noticed that he still didn't look happy about the idea.

While they carried their belongings to the porch, Maddie kept an eye on Tibby. All afternoon, the girl had been sitting in the field watching them. Maddie had wondered if Tibby would go with Reba and Tom to the Loftis place. She had been pleased, and a little surprised, when she saw that Tibby had stayed here.

Mama came out and picked up a basket filled with canned peas and beans to carry inside. She saw Maddie watching Tibby.

"Reckon that child was as bound not to be left as you were not to leave her," Mama said.

"I know you didn't want her to come," Maddie said, "but we didn't force her. She made up her own mind."

"Didn't say I didn't want her," Mama said. "Only she looks so nearly white—might cause trouble if town folks think we got a white child livin' with us."

"All I know is, we can't send her away," Maddie said firmly. "We're all she's got."

"Well, what you gonna do with her?" Mama asked.

Maddie shook her head. "Give her time, I reckon. Hope she learns not to be so scared. Don't know what else I can do."

They had just built a fire to cook supper when Daniel's wagon came into sight. He and Ruth brought fresh milk and vegetables from their garden.

Maddie ran to the wagon. She hugged Ruth and set the pitcher of milk on the makeshift table Royall and Zebedee had set up in the yard. Mama buzzed around, pulling crates up to the table for chairs and looking happy. Maddie figured this was what she'd been waiting for ever since they left the island—serving supper to neighbors at her own table.

While they ate, they talked about what they would plant. Beans, Irish potatoes, sweet potatoes, peas, muskmelons, squash, and onions. And they'd put in twenty acres of corn. Daniel told them if the crop was good, they might harvest three hundred bushels or more. They could sell half and still have plenty for roasting, making meal, and feeding the stock.

"Your family's gonna need you full-time for a while," Daniel said to Zebedee. "But once the house is fixed and the plantin's done, come see me and I'll put you to work."

"Miz Ella, I'll be out to help y'all ever' day," Ruth said. "Don't take me long to tend to our little place. And maybe, after the work's all done," she added, look-

54

ing shyly at Maddie, "you can teach me to read. Iffen you really want to."

Maddie smiled. "I really want to," she said.

"And on Sunday, we'll come get you for services," Ruth went on happily. "We don't have a real church yet, but Mister Loftis lets us use a barn on his place."

"All the colored families work for Mister Loftis?" Mama asked.

"Almost all," Daniel said. "And he's agreed to take Ben on."

"That right?" Zebedee looked surprised. "Didn't figger Ben was interested in workin' shares, with him plannin' to go out West."

"Mister Loftis sez he'll pay him cash when the crops come in," Ruth said. "And he's lettin' Ben share a cabin with the single men."

The sun was slipping behind the trees, and Ruth and Daniel were getting ready to go home, when they saw horses approaching. Three white men on horseback turned off the main road and headed for the house.

Everybody stood, watching the rapid advance of the men. Maddie felt uneasy, remembering how the folks in town had stared at them.

"It's Mister Gentry and his boy Dewey," Ruth said softly. "That's Mister Newsome with 'em."

Daniel walked out into the yard. When the men stopped their horses in front of him, Maddie saw that they didn't look friendly.

"Daniel, what's the meanin'a this?" Mister Gentry said. "You know you're not doin' the town any good bringin' in more coloreds."

"Had to bring my brother home," Daniel said. Maddie thought he sounded calm and unafraid, but *she* didn't feel that way. Her heart was beating so hard she could hear it pounding in her ears.

"Your brother and all them others," Mister Newsome said. He was looking over Daniel's head at Maddie and her family.

"Daniel, ain't we always treated you right?" Mister Gentry was speaking in a sociable way, but his face was hard. "You 'member what I told you when you moved to Willoughby way back? I said we needed somebody with your skills, and we wouldn't make trouble for you, long as you behaved yourself. I've kept my word, haven't I?"

"You have."

"You're damned right I have!" Mister Gentry said sharply. "You wouldn't have a business if we didn't give you our trade. But you've gone back on your part'a the bargain."

"What part's that, Mister Gentry?" Daniel asked in a quiet voice.

"The part about behavin' yourself." The white man's eyes were narrowed to slits. "You're bringin' in these niggers to take over our town. Now, that ain't gonna work."

Dewey Gentry, who was as tall and brawny as Daniel, was wiping at his nose and snickering at his father's words.

"We heared tell these niggers tried to buy this place from Judd Loftis," Mister Newsome added. "That right, Daniel?"

Maddie saw Daniel's head turn ever so slightly toward them. His back was as stiff as a broom handle, and Maddie realized that he wasn't feeling calm at all.

"They bought the land from Mister Loftis," Daniel said.

"It ain't legal!" Mister Newsome glared at Daniel.

"No law that says coloreds can't own land," Daniel said.

"Well, there's laws and there's the way things've always been," Mister Gentry said. "We already got too many niggers in this town thinkin' they're good as white folks, and it's time they moved on. You get my meanin', Daniel? 'Cause if you don't, I can't see how we'll be able to give you any more business. Reckon you won't have any work a-tall."

Maddie felt sick. She took a step toward Daniel, but Mama grabbed her arm and yanked her back.

Mister Gentry sat up tall in his saddle, frowning, his eyes sliding over Maddie and the others, one by one. " 'Less you're lookin' for trouble, you best get back in that wagon'a yours and move on," he said.

Dewey snickered again and his father gave him a sharp look. "We've wasted enough time for one day," he said and slapped the reins against his horse's side.

They left as quickly as they had come, the horses' hooves pounding the dirt as they headed back to the road. When Maddie looked around at the faces of her family, she could see the same fear and despair that she was feeling.

"Mama, I told you we shouldn't of left the island," Angeline said in a small voice.

"I reckon we coulda waited and been run off," Mama said sharply.

"What you 'spect they'll do if we don't leave?" Zebedee wondered.

"Bad as he is, I've never knowed Mister Gentry to use violence against nobody," Daniel said. He looked from Zebedee to Mama to Maddie. "This land belongs to you. Can't nobody run you off it."

Mama placed her hand on Daniel's arm. "You and Ruth've done more for me and my family than we had any right to expect," she said gently. "We don't wanta be the cause of you losin' ever'thing you worked for."

Daniel covered her hand with his. "Miz Ella, no matter what Mister Gentry said, there's always gonna be harnesses that need fixin' and folks with holes in their shoes. You don't fret none over Ruth and me. Looks like you got your hands full just patchin' up this old place."

Maddie was sure she would be too worried to sleep. But when she and Zebedee spread their quilts out on the porch, weariness washed over her and she couldn't keep her eyes open.

Later, she awoke to the sound of rain tapping on the porch roof, and her first thought was of Tibby. Maddie pictured the child huddled wet and miserable in the field. She knew she had to try to coax her in out of the rain.

Maddie lit a lantern and pulled a shawl over her head. She started down the steps—then stopped.

At the end of the porch, as far away from Maddie's and Zebedee's pallets as possible, Tibby lay curled up like a sleeping cat. In the soft light from the lantern, Maddie could see that the girl's eyes were closed and that she was completely dry.

Maddie smiled. She picked up her quilt and moved to where Tibby slept. Gently, so as not to wake her,

Maddie covered the child and returned to the other end of the porch. When she looked back, she saw that the girl's eyes were open. They stared at each other for a moment. Then Tibby snuggled in under the quilt and, with a catlike yawn, closed her eyes again.

8

Brother Isaac was a tall, gangly young man with a generous smile. He stood outside the barn speaking to folks as they arrived for Sunday services. He pressed the women's hands gently between both of his own and slapped the men on the back. He listened and nodded, and sometimes, he threw his head back and laughed.

When Ruth introduced Maddie and her family to Brother Isaac, he stretched out his arms as though to draw them all to him. "We's most heartily glad to have you with us," he said. "Praise the Lord for bringin' you here safely." Then he shook everyone's hand, including Pride's, and offered welcoming words with each handshake. Maddie walked into church feeling that she already belonged there.

Sunlight streamed through loose and missing boards, casting a glow on the rough pine benches and the faces of the congregation. Although the barn no longer sheltered horses and cows, the sweet smells of animals and damp hay filled Maddie's nostrils.

When everyone was seated, Brother Isaac strode to the makeshift pulpit and the chatter around Maddie stopped. All eyes were focused on the young preacher.

"Brothers and Sisters," he began in a quiet voice, "rejoice in all the Lord has given us—our families, the fruits of our labor, the circle of friends we's worshipin' with today." Then his smile turned to a grin and his eyes glowed with excitement as he bellowed, "Yes, *rejoice!* Rejoice in humility and gladness for the Lord's deliverance. Jehovah's triumphed! His peoples is free!"

The folks around Maddie cried out "Amen!" and "Praise the Lord!"

"In the Old Testament, we's told that the Lord brung his people outta Egypt—"

"Amen!" the congregation cried.

"Where they wuz kept in bondage. And the Lord brung 'em forth with a mighty hand."

"With a mighty hand!"

"And he brung 'em to a free land!" Brother Isaac shouted.

"A free land! Hallelujah!"

"A land that flows with milk and honey."

"Amen!" the congregation cried.

"And the people gathered the fruits of their labor from this sweet land and rejoiced in their deliverance. Yes, they rejoiced!"

When his sermon was finished, Brother Isaac led the congregation in hymns. Joyfully, they sang, "Blow Ye the Trumpet, Blow," "O Freedom Over Me," and "Michael, Haul the Boat Ashore"—songs Maddie knew from the island church. Then they sang a hymn she had never heard before. Tears filled Maddie's eyes as the voices around her swelled with the words of freedom and peace.

Deep River, my home is over Jordan;
Deep River, my home is over Jordan.
O don't you want to go to that Gospel Feast,
That Promised Land where all is Peace?
Deep River, I want to cross over.

61

That was all her family wanted, Maddie thought. To be free and to live in peace.

After services, Brother Isaac shook hands and slapped backs all over again. When he asked Pride what he thought of the sermon, Pride said, "It surely was loud." Mama looked mortified and jerked on Pride's arm, but Brother Isaac just laughed.

As they walked to the wagon, Angeline asked why William hadn't come to services.

"He weren't feelin' good," Ruth said.

"Or else him and Ben wuz goin' fishin'," Daniel said.

Ruth gave her brother a disapproving look, but before she could scold him, Daniel added, "Brother Isaac sez he's found us a teacher."

Ruth's face lit up at that. "He has? Tell us about her, Daniel. What's her name? Where's she from? Or is it a he?"

"Take a breath, sister," Daniel demanded, but he was smiling. "She's a young colored woman from Ohio, name'a Jane Woods. Just outta teacher's college."

"Teacher's college," Ruth repeated softly. "I never knowed a colored person that went to college."

Maddie was as excited by the news as Ruth. The teacher might have books she could borrow. Books read by folks who'd been to college! And she was from the North. Maddie knew from her studies with Miz James that Ohio had always been a free state. The new teacher could tell Maddie what it was like to live as a free colored person up North.

"When's she comin'?" Maddie asked.

"Brother Isaac sez she'll be here in a couple weeks," Daniel said. "For right now, we'll have to use this old barn for the school, but someday we'll have us a new church *and* a new school."

As they drove home, Mama asked Daniel, "How's business been this week?"

"Fair to middlin'."

"Daniel, I want a straight answer," Mama said in her no-nonsense voice.

"It's dropped off some," Daniel admitted. "But I reckon not ever'body's listenin' to Owen Gentry, 'cause some folks is still bringin' me work. Mister Loftis come in twice this week."

"Don't Mister Loftis have his own folks to do leather work?" Ruth asked.

"He does," Daniel said.

"You reckon Mister Gentry talked to Mister Loftis about sellin' us land?" Royall asked.

"No doubt in my mind," Daniel said. "I 'spect he chewed Mister Loftis up one side and down the other."

"Well, it sounds like his chewin' fell on deaf ears," Mama said.

Next morning, they went back to working on the house. Maddie scrubbed the floors with sand and water. She cleaned the window glass with vinegar, and they all marveled at how bright the house was with sunlight pouring in. Zebedee cleaned the chimney and Royall built a new ladder to the sleeping loft. Mama and Angeline washed quilts and hung sheer muslin curtains they had made for the island house. They hadn't been able to bring much furniture from the island, but Mama's good rocker was set near the fireplace, and Royall and Zebedee built a pine table and benches for the front room.

When work on the house was finished, Zebedee took a scythe to the tall grass around the house and barn.

Then he helped Royall fence in the barn lot. The day they finished the fencing, Royall went to see Mister Loftis and brought home a Guernsey cow and four chickens. Everyone came out when they saw Royall drive in with the cow tied to the wagon.

Angeline peered at the animal. "That's about the scrawniest cow I ever did see. Reckon she'll even give milk?"

"The Loftis boy told me what livestock the Confederate Army didn't take, the Union soldiers did," Royall said. "Reckon we's lucky to have any cow a-tall."

Maddie looked into the animal's sad brown eyes and stroked her neck. "Don't you listen to 'em," she murmured. "We'll fatten you up and you'll be the prettiest cow in North Carolina."

Zebedee chortled. "Next you'll be wantin' to tie a ribbon 'round her neck and parade her through town."

"Maybe I just will," Maddie said. "And I reckon I'll call her Pretty Girl, so she'll get the idea what she's supposed to grow up to be."

Mama shook her head. "Since you'll be the one milkin' her, you can call her anything you want."

When the plowing and planting started, everybody pitched in. Royall pushed the plow through the hard earth, while Zebedee led the mule. Day after day, the sound of Royall's voice carried across the field. "C'mon, mule!" he'd yell. "Don't be quittin' on me now. Haw!"

Mama, Angeline, and Maddie followed behind the plow with their seed sacks, the white sun beating down on their bonnets. Angeline carried Elizabeth strapped to her back. While she dropped seeds in the plowed rows and used her hoe to cover them with dirt, Angeline talked to the baby and sang silly songs. Elizabeth's favorite was the corn-planting rhyme.

One for the blackbird
One for the crow
One for the cutworm
And two to grow.

Angeline bounced on "two to grow," and Elizabeth shrieked with laughter.

Almost every day, Ruth came out to the farm driving Daniel's wagon. She'd leave the flowers or bread she brought in the house, tie on her bonnet, and join them in the fields. One day, Ruth stopped to mop the sweat off her face and noticed Tibby sitting under a tree near the house.

"She come out in the daytime now?" Ruth asked Maddie.

"Sometimes," Maddie said. "She'll disappear for the longest time; then I'll look up and there she is."

"She let you touch her?"

Maddie shook her head. "But she's not as scared as she was. 'Fore winter, I've got to figger out how to get her into the house."

Ruth looked doubtful. "Reckon that'll take a miracle," she said.

But Maddie could tell that Tibby was becoming more comfortable with them. At night she'd go to the porch and curl up on her quilt before the rest of them had gone to bed. Maddie could leave the child's plate on the porch steps and Tibby would come out in broad daylight to get it. That morning, Tibby had even shown up in the barn while Maddie was milking Pretty Girl. Maddie didn't say anything to the girl—she just kept on milking and talking to the cow—but out of the corner of her eye, she saw Tibby move closer and closer, and finally, sit down in a pile of hay to watch.

After supper dishes were done, Maddie and Angeline went out to the porch to cool off. The sun had gone down and darkness was gathering, but the day's heat still hovered around them. Maddie sat on the steps, fanning herself with her apron.

"Won't help," Angeline said. "You're just stirrin' up hot air."

Maddie stopped fanning. Her back ached from stooping all day. She stretched and leaned back on her elbows. "Royall says we'll be done with the plantin' tomorrow or the next day," she said.

"Then the weedin' begins," Angeline said. "Then the pickin'. And next spring we start all over."

Maddie smiled. "Reckon ownin' land's a mixed blessin'."

Zebedee and Pride had just come out to sit with them when Maddie heard a sound like far-off thunder. "Could sure use a rain to cool things off," she said.

But then the dull rumble grew louder and she realized that it wasn't thunder—it was the sound of horses on the road.

Maddie stood up. In the growing darkness, she could see the narrow ribbon of road broken by shadows. And she could see horsemen moving rapidly toward the house.

Maddie pulled Pride up from the steps. "Ever'body get inside," she said sharply.

"What's wrong?" Pride sounded scared.

66

"Just go inside," Maddie said, pushing him toward the door.

Royall was there when they slammed the door shut. He was holding his rifle and peering out the front window. "Could you see how many there is?" he asked.

"Too dark," Maddie said. "Might be a dozen—maybe more."

Mama was coming out of the storeroom, wiping her hands on a kitchen rag. She saw them huddled around the window and looked puzzled. Then her eyes fell on the rifle. "Royall, what's happenin'?"

"Riders, Miz Ella. They's comin' here."

Mama looked stunned.

"Blow out them lights," Royall said.

Zebedee moved quickly to the candles on the table and mantle and blew them out.

The pounding of hooves moved closer. Maddie put her arms around Pride and pulled him to her. She could feel the fear in his small, tense body. Then she remembered Tibby. Royall caught her arm as she ran to the door.

"Where you think you're goin'?" he demanded.

"Tibby's out there," Maddie said.

Royall pulled her hand from the doorknob. "She'll hide till they's gone."

"But—"

"You can't go out there," Royall said firmly. "Now you all move away from the door."

Mama pulled Angeline and Pride into a corner. Maddie stooped down beside the window. All she could see outside was darkness, but the sound grew louder as the horses neared the house. Then Maddie saw a point of light like the glow of a firefly. Then another light. And another.

"They got torches," Royall said softly.

Fear shot through Maddie's body, making her feel cold and weak. She could see the string of torches moving toward them. The horses and riders were nothing more than dark smudges against the darker field, but the flames seemed to leap out of the night at her.

Tibby would be terrified, Maddie thought. She'd remember the last time horsemen came with torches. Maddie clenched her fists and prayed that Tibby would stay hidden.

The horses circled the house and the earth trembled, causing dishes and window glass to rattle. Shouts from the men rose above the roar. Maddie couldn't make out the words, but she could hear the anger and frenzy in their voices. Each time the riders sped past the window, flames flashing in the glass, Maddie feared they had set the porch on fire.

Then she realized that the horses were slowing and the shouting was dying down. One by one, the riders came to the front of the house and stopped. The silence was more frightening than the noise had been.

Zebedee slid across the floor to Maddie. "Get away from the window," he whispered. But before she could respond, the window exploded. Shards of glass flew across the room and Elizabeth's screams pierced the darkness. Zebedee pushed Maddie to the floor.

Through the broken window, Maddie could hear the men shouting again. "Get outta town!" they yelled. "You ain't welcome here!"

Maddie lay on the floor with Zebedee's arm around her—trying to shut out the hate-filled voices—for what

68

seemed like an endless time. Until finally the shouting stopped and Maddie could hear the men riding away.

Mama lit candles. Pride was hanging on to her skirt, sniffling and wiping away tears. Angeline paced the floor with a wailing Elizabeth in her arms.

"You been hurt," Zebedee said to Maddie. He pointed to the trickle of blood that ran down her arm.

Maddie got to her feet and headed for the door. Her legs felt weak, like they might buckle under her.

"Maddie, where you goin'?" Mama demanded.

"To see about Tibby."

"Let me bind your arm," Mama said.

But Maddie didn't seem to hear her. She lit the lantern and hurried outside.

Maddie walked across the yard calling Tibby's name, over and over. She didn't expect the girl to answer, but still she called.

"They're gone, Tibby," Maddie called into the darkness. "Come on out now."

Maddie searched the yard and the fields, calling for Tibby until she was hoarse. As time passed and there was still no sign of the child, Maddie's worry grew. What if Tibby had panicked and taken off across the fields? What if she had run so far she didn't know how to get back? If she was out of earshot, how would they ever find her?

Maddie headed for the barn, walking faster, her calls more frantic.

"Tibby, answer me! I know you can hear me." In fact, Maddie didn't know that at all, and she was frightened.

She opened the barn door. The light from the lantern fell on Pretty Girl's face, then on the mules in their stalls.

"Tibby!"

Maddie searched every corner of the stalls and feed bins. Then she started up the ladder to the hayloft.

"Tibby, are you here?"

When she reached the top of the ladder, Maddie held the lantern up and the soft light spread across the empty loft. That's when she saw her.

Tibby was huddled in a far corner. Her eyes were huge, and her knees were drawn up tightly to her chin.

Feeling weak with relief, Maddie set the lantern down and climbed slowly into the loft. Tibby pressed her body against the wall.

"Tibby, you're safe," Maddie said softly. "They're gone now. There's nothin' to be scared of."

Maddie was squatting a few feet from the child. She began to inch slowly toward Tibby. As Maddie moved closer, Tibby's eyes darted around the loft, looking for a way out. But Maddie blocked her path to the ladder.

"I won't hurt you," Maddie said. "It's all right, Tibby."

Maddie was close enough to touch the child when Tibby sprang to her feet. She tried to dive past Maddie, but Maddie caught her around the waist.

Tibby screamed. She fought and kicked, striking Maddie in the chest. Maddie fell back, but she didn't loosen her hold on the child.

They wrestled on the floor. The girl was so small and skinny, Maddie was shocked by her strength.

Tibby fought and struggled and screeched until she was exhausted. Maddie held on, her arms so tired they were beginning to feel numb. She was wondering how much longer she could hold the girl when Tibby finally stopped fighting.

They were both breathing hard. Tibby lay on her back, staring up at Maddie. In the soft light, Maddie had her first up-close look at the child. At the thin, pointed face and the large brown eyes still filled with fear. And Maddie could see the golden tint to her pale skin, the blend of her mama's blood and that of the white man.

Maddie studied the small face—the raised chin and the steady gaze—and was filled with admiration. Yes, Tibby was scared, but she was also brave. She had fought as hard as she could, and even now, pinned down by someone so much bigger and stronger, she wouldn't give up. Maddie knew that as soon as she got the chance, Tibby would fight again. She'd bolt from the loft and lose herself in the darkness unless Maddie did something to stop her.

"I know you're scared," Maddie said to the girl, "but you can't go on runnin' wild. I won't let you."

Tibby grunted and tried to jerk her arms free, but her eyes never left Maddie's.

"You know what I'm sayin'?" Maddie asked softly. "You're safe with me. I reckon you don't believe that yet. All you know to do is run. But I won't let you go. I'm keepin' you here and I'm gonna take care'a you. No more livin' in the woods and fields."

Maddie talked like this for a long time. Gradually, she felt some of the tension leave Tibby's body.

"We won't let anybody hurt you," Maddie told her. "I know you been watchin' my family and me—you see how we take care'a one another. Now we're gonna take care'a you. And tonight, you won't be sleepin' on the porch. You'll sleep in the house with me."

Tibby's breathing came faster and she stiffened.

"I 'spect that scares you some, but you'll like it once you get used to it," Maddie went on in the same soft voice. "There's a sleepin' loft in the house. Zebedee and Pride have a room up there, and you and me have ours. Nobody'll bother you, Tibby. You'll be safe."

It was very late when Maddie came to the house with Tibby in her arms. Nobody had gone to bed. They all sat in the front room, waiting.

Tibby's body grew rigid when Maddie carried her into the house. Her eyes moved fearfully from one surprised face to another, and she pressed hard against Maddie.

"See that ladder," Maddie said as they walked into the front room. "Up there's where we sleep."

She carried Tibby to the ladder. "Grab hold and go on up," Maddie said. "I'll be right behind you."

Tibby hesitated. Then she grasped one of the rungs and climbed into the loft.

The family watched as Maddie followed the child up the ladder.

"Well, I'll be," Mama whispered.

9

Next morning, Maddie was feeding the chickens when she saw Daniel's wagon coming up the road to the house. She threw down the last of the cracked corn and went to meet him. Pride, who had been gathering eggs, ran after her.

"Come to see if y'all wuz all right," Daniel said as he pulled the wagon to a stop. "Some men rode over to the Loftis cabins last night swingin' torches and threatenin' folks."

"They came here, too," Maddie said.

"Busted out the window," Pride said in a grave voice.

"Anybody hurt?" Daniel asked quickly.

Maddie shook her head. "Just scared. We couldn't see their faces, but I reckon we all know who's behind it."

Daniel climbed down from the wagon. "Maddie, you best be keepin' them kind'a thoughts to yourself. Don't wanta make it sound like you're accusin' somebody."

"I *am* accusin' somebody," Maddie said. "Mister Gentry and his no-good friends, that's who."

Mama had come out on the porch. She gave Maddie a look of warning, then turned to Daniel. "You had breakfast yet?" she asked him. "Come on in and I'll serve you up some hot biscuits and bacon."

"Much obliged," Daniel said.

Pride followed Daniel into the house, but Maddie headed to the barn. There were still chores to do before they went to the fields. She found Tibby sitting on the barn-lot fence.

"Where'd you get off to so early?" Maddie asked her. "When I woke up, you were gone."

Tibby didn't respond, but neither did she run when Maddie came to stand beside her.

"I'll bet you're hungry," Maddie said. "I set you a place at the table—too bad you weren't there to eat."

Tibby looked puzzled.

"You'll be eatin' at the table with us from now on," Maddie said. "I won't be settin' food on the steps for you anymore."

Tibby scowled.

"When you're hungry, come inside and I'll feed you," Maddie said. "You understand?"

Tibby folded her arms across her chest and stared hard at Maddie.

Maddie tried not to smile. The child might not be talking, but she was showing how she felt plain enough. "I gotta strain the milk; then I'm goin' up to the house. If you come with me, I'll give you breakfast."

Maddie poured the milk through a clean cloth to separate it from the cream. When she carried the buckets to the house, Tibby trailed behind her. But when they reached the porch, the child refused to go inside.

"There's hot biscuits with butter and molasses," Maddie said. "And bacon and fried apples."

Tibby's struggle with herself showed on her face. She peered into the house as though wanting to follow Maddie through the door, then clamped her lips together and stubbornly refused to move further than the steps.

"It's up to you," Maddie said. "We're goin' to the fields—this'll be your last chance to eat till supper."

Leaving the door open, Maddie went inside. Daniel was sitting at the table finishing his breakfast. Royall sat on the hearth sanding a square of wood to replace the broken windowpane.

Maddie poured the cream into the churn. "Reckon we'll ever be able to afford another piece'a glass?" she asked.

"Maybe when the corn's sold," Royall said.

Mama and Pride came from the storeroom with corn cakes and sweet potatoes. Mama began to pack the dinner bucket to take to the field. "You reckon those men just meant to throw a scare into us?" she asked Daniel.

"Looks that way," he said. "Nobody wuz hurt at the Loftis place neither. If they'd been out to do real harm ..." Daniel glanced at Pride and didn't finish. But they all knew what he was thinking: If the men had wanted to harm them, nobody would have been able to stop them.

"Don't know what to do," Mama said. "Maybe they'll get used to us bein' here and settle down—and maybe they won't."

"This is our home," Royall said in a quiet voice.

"It is," Maddie said. She was about to say more, but then she looked up and saw Tibby standing by the door glaring at her. Maddie filled a plate and placed it on the table.

Tibby hesitated, her eyes moving from the plate to the faces around her.

"Reckon we best be gettin' to the field 'fore the sun's too high," Mama said softly.

As they left, Maddie saw Tibby edge toward the table and reach for a biscuit.

When the planting was finished, Royall and Zebedee began to cut trees for Royall and Angeline's house. Daniel helped them load the logs on the wagon to take to the sawmill. Maddie and Angeline ran out to meet them when they came back.

"Will you look at that," Maddie said in wonderment when she saw the load of straight, smooth boards on the back of the wagon.

Angeline beamed and held Elizabeth up to see. "Look what fine lumber your papa's brought for our house," she said.

Royall drove the wagon to the crest of the hill that overlooked the pond. While the men pounded posts into the ground to mark off two rooms, Maddie, Angeline, and Pride began to gather smooth stones for the fireplace.

Tibby was never far from Maddie's side now. During the day, she followed Maddie through the fields and back and forth to the barn, waiting patiently until Maddie had finished her work. At mealtime, Tibby slipped in after everyone else was seated and took her place at the end of the bench next to Maddie. She kept her eyes on her plate while she ate, but Maddie knew she watched them all the while. At bedtime, Tibby was the first one to scramble up the ladder. By the time Maddie came to bed, Tibby was already curled up on the small mattress that Mama had made for her.

By the end of the week, the walls of the house were

up, and a mound of stones had been gathered for the fireplace. Maddie dumped an apronload of stones on the pile and sat down next to Angeline to rest.

"Maddie, look," Angeline said.

Maddie's gaze followed Angeline's across the field. She saw Tibby walking slowly with her eyes to the ground. Then the child stooped down, disappearing into the tall grass. When Tibby popped up and began to walk again, Maddie asked, "What's she doin'?"

"Pickin' up stones," Angeline said. And Maddie smiled.

When the house was finished, they loaded mattresses and pots and Elizabeth's cradle on the wagon and carried them up the hill.

"We'll make curtains," Mama said. "And after the harvest, we'll piece a new quilt."

Maddie sat on the front steps looking out over the apple trees and the pond and her house. Tibby ran through the grass, stopping occasionally to pick wildflowers. She had a fistful of white spring beauties and purple passion flowers.

"Pretty flowers," Maddie called to her.

Tibby looked at Maddie, then at the flowers, and a tiny smile began to tug at her lips.

When they arrived for church services the first Sunday in July, Maddie saw a young woman standing with Brother Isaac. She was wearing a hat with pink ribbons, and she held a pale blue parasol to shade her face from the sun. Maddie had never seen a colored woman carry a parasol. This had to be the new teacher.

"Maddie, come meet Miz Woods!" Ruth hurried over to Maddie and grabbed her hand. "She's nice," Ruth whispered. "And so smart and pretty. Puts me in mind of you."

Ruth pulled Maddie through the crowd and introduced her to the teacher.

Jane Woods smiled and reached for Maddie's hand. "It's so nice to meet you, Maddie," she said in a gentle voice that made Maddie think of Miz James. "Ruth's been telling me about you, and I was hoping you might be able to help me with the school."

Jane Woods didn't look much older than Maddie and Ruth, but her elegant clothing and refined speech made Maddie feel shy. "I'd be pleased to help," she said softly.

"Perhaps you'd have time to look at the books I brought before classes begin next week," the teacher said. "I've never taught before and I'd appreciate your ideas on which texts to use."

The mention of books brought a smile to Maddie's face. "I'd like that, Miz Woods."

"Outside of school, why don't you and Ruth call me Jane?" the teacher suggested. "I'm not used to being called Miz Woods. Besides, I hope we'll all become friends."

Suddenly Maddie realized that, despite her fancy clothes and education, Jane Woods was also feeling shy. Maddie hadn't stopped to think what it would be like to come to a strange place without friends or family.

After church services, Mama invited Jane and Brother Isaac home for Sunday dinner. Since Ruth and Daniel were also invited, Ruth followed Jane to the Henry wagon.

"Where you livin'?" Ruth asked Jane.

"Mister Loftis was kind enough to let me stay in one of his cabins."

Maddie was shocked to hear this. She couldn't picture the elegant young teacher in a slave cabin. "Must be real different from what you're used to," she said.

Jane smiled. "Brother Isaac had it fixed up nice for me."

Maddie was eyeing the rose-colored brooch on the teacher's crisp white shirtwaist. "Still, it must be different. Were you born in Ohio?"

Jane nodded. "My father owns a barber shop in Oberlin, Ohio. That's where my three brothers and I grew up."

"Brother Isaac sez you been to college," Ruth said.

"Oberlin College," Jane replied. "Two of my brothers graduated from Oberlin before me. One's a school administrator in New York; the other's a lawyer." She smiled. "My little brother, Luke, says he wants to go to California and pan for gold, but if Mother has anything to say about it, he'll go to Oberlin, too."

"I never knew colored folks could go to college," Maddie said. "Ohio must be a good place to live."

"We didn't have slavery, but most whites in Ohio don't see colored people as their equals," Jane said. "Oberlin's the only college I know of that accepts colored students, and there weren't many of us."

"Your mama and papa must be proud of you," Maddie said.

Jane smiled, but she looked sad. "Actually, they're disappointed. They were afraid for me to come here so soon after the war. But I want to do something that matters." Suddenly the sadness was gone and her eyes were shining. "When I read about children in the South who'd never been taught to read and write, I knew I had to come."

Maddie's heart thumped hard against her ribs. Here was someone else who wanted to do something important with her life, and she hadn't let anything stand in her way.

"I know how you feel," Maddie said.

Jane studied Maddie's face thoughtfully. "Perhaps you'll tell me about that sometime."

Maddie was making a blackberry pie for supper when she heard Pride yell from the porch, "Daniel's here! Wait till you see what he's got."

Maddie looked at Tibby, who was sitting at the table eating blackberries. Purple juice ran down her chin and the front of her shift. "You reckon we better go see what the hollerin's about?" she asked.

Maddie went to the porch and Tibby followed. Pride was in the back of Daniel's wagon. He was grinning.

"Come on, Maddie," Pride said. "Come see."

Daniel was smiling as he watched Pride.

"What's all the to-do?" Maddie asked as she walked over to the wagon. Then she saw that Pride had his arms around something—something that moved.

It was a dog. A big sandy-colored dog, which licked Pride's face and sent him into a fit of giggles.

Maddie turned to look at Tibby, wondering if she would be frightened by the animal. But Tibby was staring at the dog in fascination without a hint of fear in her eyes.

"Daniel calls him Jubal," Pride said between giggles.

"We need us a dog, Maddie. Reckon Mama'd let us have one?"

The dog turned his head to look at Maddie as though waiting for her answer.

Mama and Angeline had come out on the porch.

"Daniel, where'd you get that ugly critter?" Mama called.

"Just showed up at the house yesterday," Daniel said.

"And you fed him," Mama said in an accusing voice.

Daniel looked sheepish. "Couldn't turn away a starvin' animal, Miz Ella."

Mama frowned. "So what's he doin' here?"

"Glad you asked, Miz Ella," Daniel said. "I wuz thinkin' how with you livin' out here by yourselves, you could do with a good watchdog. I wuz thinkin'—"

"Daniel, you rascal, just climb back in your wagon and take that dog on outta here," Mama said.

"Oh, Mama," Pride wailed. "Can't we keep him? Please?"

Mama was scowling at Daniel. "I've a good mind to take a strap to you," she said.

"Didn't mean to make trouble," Daniel said contritely, but Maddie could see the smile in his eyes.

Maddie looked at Mama. She was still scowling.

"Dog that big can *eat*," Mama muttered.

"He's not *that* big," Maddie said.

"Now, don't you start," Mama said sharply. She stared at the dog, who was happily bathing Pride's face again.

"Reckon he could sleep on the porch," Angeline said. "Warn us when somebody's comin'."

"Haven't heard him bark once," Mama grumbled. "Bet that dog don't even know how to bark."

81

"Oh, he barks, Miz Ella," Daniel said.

"I'll take care of him," Pride said in a small voice.

"You surely will," Mama said. "With all I got to do, I don't have time to mess with no dog."

Pride shouted and leaped out of the wagon. The dog bounded out after him. Maddie could see now that he *was* a big dog, but he had a sweet face and his sides were sunken in like he'd missed a lot of meals. She stroked his head and he licked her hand.

When she looked back at the porch, Maddie saw that Angeline was trying not to laugh and Mama wasn't scowling quite so hard.

And Tibby was smiling.

10

Maddie made several trips to the pond, carrying back buckets of water to heat on the fire. Tibby trailed behind her. When the water was heated, Maddie carried it to the storeroom and poured it into the washtub. Tibby watched while Maddie collected a cake of soap, cotton rags, a sheet, and a comb. But when Maddie closed Tibby and herself up in the storeroom, Tibby began to get suspicious.

"It's time you had a bath," Maddie said.

Tibby looked at the tub of water and then at Maddie.

"You want me to help you undress?" Maddie started to lift the filthy shift over Tibby's head, and Tibby made a run for the door. Maddie caught her before she could open it.

"A little soap and water's not gonna hurt you," Maddie said. She struggled to get the girl's shift off with one hand and held Tibby with the other. Maddie wasn't surprised when Tibby wailed and struggled to get away.

"There now." Maddie threw the dirty clothing to the floor. She picked up a squirming, unhappy Tibby and carried her to the tub.

This is getting easier, Maddie thought, as she lowered the girl into the warm water. But as soon as Tibby's body touched the water, the girl let out a screech and started fighting as hard as ever.

"No, no, no," Maddie said under her breath as she fended off Tibby's flailing arms and fought to keep her in the tub. "You can't come out till you're clean."

A swell of water hit Maddie in the face. She struggled blindly to hold on to Tibby while wiping her eyes.

Tibby screamed and kicked and splashed. Maddie figured the only thing to do was wait. She sat on the floor holding Tibby in the tub until the girl had worn herself out.

When Tibby was finally still, Maddie said, "If you don't fight me, we'll be done in no time. But either way, I'm gonna give you a bath and wash your hair."

Tibby glared at her and raised a hand as though to strike out again.

Maddie gave the child a warning look. Slowly, Tibby lowered her hand back into the water. She stuck her bottom lip out as far as it would go and turned her face away.

"I know," Maddie said. "You're mad at me. You don't like this a bit, do you? Well, that's all right, but you're still gettin' a bath."

Maddie scrubbed the little body with a soapy cloth. She could see now how very thin the child was. When Maddie poured water from a bucket over Tibby's hair, being careful not to get it in her eyes, Tibby groaned as though Maddie were causing her great pain.

After sudsing and rinsing Tibby's hair several times, Maddie said, "Reckon that'll do it."

She lifted the child from the tub, wrapped her in a sheet, and carried her into the front room. Sitting down in Mama's rocker with Tibby in her lap, Maddie squeezed water out of the girl's hair and began to pull a comb through it. When the comb caught in tangles, Tibby scowled at Maddie, but she didn't try to run away.

That afternoon, Ruth came to visit. Maddie was sitting on the porch sewing on one of her old dresses for Tibby. Standing in the yard at a safe distance, Tibby watched Pride romp with the dog. She was wearing a shirt of Pride's, which fell below her knees.

Ruth was still staring at Tibby when she climbed the steps to the porch. "Heavens, Maddie, whad you do to that child? She's turnin' out plumb pretty."

Maddie looked across the yard at Tibby and nodded. Now that it was clean, the yellow hair was as pale as cornsilk and curled softly around Tibby's face—a face with even features and great, dark eyes that were filled with liveliness and curiosity. Tibby was more than pretty, Maddie decided; she was beautiful.

Ruth sat down and touched the dress in Maddie's lap. "That's a nice print," Ruth said.

Maddie shook out the dress and held it up. Tiny pink flowers covered the light brown background. There was lace at the throat and pearl buttons down the front.

"This was the first store-bought dress I ever had," Maddie said. "Came in a missionary barrel our first Christmas on Roanoke Island. I can't tell you how much I loved this dress, Ruth. Wore it to services every Sunday till it was way too short and tight."

Ruth stroked the fabric. "And now you're makin' it over for Tibby."

Maddie smiled and went back to her sewing.

"I saw Zebedee 'fore I left," Ruth said. "Daniel has him and William workin' in the shop."

"They doin' all right?"

"Zebedee's workin' hard," Ruth said. "But I'm worried 'bout William. I wuz hopin' he'd be happy once we got him home, but he's so angry! And him and Daniel don't get on any better than they ever did."

"If William works hard and Daniel's proud of him, that'll ease things, don't you reckon?"

"But William ain't workin' hard," Ruth said. "Sez he hates leather work. And he's mad at Daniel 'cause Daniel won't let Ben stay with us. Daniel sez Ben oughta be at the Loftis cabins since he works for Mister Loftis, but William figgers Daniel's just bein' mean."

Maddie studied Ruth's worried face. "You want Ben to stay with you?"

"No," Ruth said emphatically. "He's bad for William. Always eggin' him on. And he gets William to sneak off when they both oughta be workin'. I blamed Daniel for him and William not gettin' along, but I tell you, Maddie, I'm near as put out with William as Daniel is."

When Maddie started out for the Loftis cabins to see Jane Woods, Tibby went with her. The child was wearing her new pink and brown dress and looking pleased with herself.

"Tibby, it's a long walk 'cross the fields," Maddie said. "I'll be back soon. Why don't you stay home and look after Jubal?"

Tibby ignored her and kept on walking.

Maddie shook her head. What a stubborn little soul she was, Maddie thought. Then she remembered all the times Mama had said the same thing about her.

"Well, suit yourself," Maddie said.

86

Children were playing in front of the cabins, but they stopped to stare when Maddie and Tibby arrived. Maddie asked a little girl where the new teacher lived, and the child pointed to the last cabin in the row.

Jane's face lit up when she opened the door and saw Maddie. Then her eyes fell on Tibby, who was hiding behind Maddie. "Who's this?" Jane asked Maddie.

"This is Tibby," Maddie said. "She lives with us now. Tibby, you wanta come inside?"

Tibby just stared at Jane and didn't move.

"Perhaps she'd feel better staying outside," Jane said. She smiled at Tibby. "We'll leave the door open, so you can keep an eye on Maddie," she said to the child.

Maddie was startled by how different Jane's cabin looked from any other slave cabin she'd seen. Two kerosene lamps glowed on a table in the center of the room, wiping out the gloom of the windowless cabin. Books were stacked on the table and on wooden crates that lined one wall. Fine skirts and shirtwaists and bonnets hung from hooks on the wall, and the pale blue parasol stood in the corner.

Jane pulled out one of the two straight-back chairs at the table and Maddie sat down. Her eyes were already devouring the books before her. She recognized some of the authors from the hours she'd spent in Master McCartha's library—supposedly cleaning, but doing a lot more looking than dusting. Mama had taught Maddie and Angeline to read when they were little girls, but she'd warned Maddie *never* to take down any of Master's books. Maddie had obeyed her mama, but she had memorized most of the titles and authors on those thin leather spines.

"Shakespeare," Maddie said, touching a dark red book.

Jane looked very surprised. "You've read William Shakespeare?"

"No," Maddie admitted. "Miz James, my teacher on the island, talked about him. And I used to see his name in my master's library. But I've read this," she said, picking up another volume.

The Last of the Mohicans." Jane smiled. "Isn't James Fenimore Cooper a wonderful writer? Have you read *Leatherstocking Tales?*"

Maddie nodded.

"And *Jane Eyre?*"

Maddie's face lit up. "Oh, yes. It's one'a my favorites. That and *The House of the Seven Gables.*"

Jane stared at Maddie. "You know Hawthorne, too? Goodness, Maddie, you've read books I didn't even know about until I went to college."

"That so?" It was Maddie's turn to be surprised.

"Truly," Jane said. "I'll loan you my books. Any you want to read. But first we have to select the ones we'll use in class."

Before Maddie left, Jane handed her two books.

"These are my favorite novels, Maddie. I'd like you to read them first so we can talk about them."

Maddie stroked the soft bindings and read the titles. One was called *The Traducer, a Historical Romance* and the other was titled *Caste.*

"When Mister Mitchell's *Caste* was published before the war, it caused quite a stir," Jane said. "It's about a governess on a Southern plantation who becomes engaged to the son of her employer. But then it's discovered that she's the daughter of a slave woman. You see, she didn't look colored so no one knew."

Like Tibby, Maddie thought.

Since most of the children were needed in the fields during the day, Jane Woods held classes in the evenings. There were nineteen children in the school, including Pride and George and Letty Spivey. When Maddie and Pride left for classes the first day, Tibby went with them.

Pride glanced at Tibby as they walked. "Maddie, I don't reckon she'll be able to read," Pride said. "She can't even talk."

"Tibby doesn't talk yet," Maddie said, "but maybe she will someday. And even if she doesn't, she can still learn to read."

"Maybe so," Pride said, but he looked doubtful.

When they arrived at the Loftis barn, the other children stared at Tibby. "That be a white girl?" a little boy asked Maddie.

"Her name's Tibby," Maddie said, "and she's no different from you and me."

"But why's she got yaller hair?" the boy persisted.

Tibby backed away, looking at the ground.

"All right, children, time for school," Jane called out. "Let's all go inside."

The children poured into the barn, forgetting about Tibby as they raced to their seats.

"Tibby, you're welcome to come inside," Jane said gently. "Or you can stay out here and listen."

Maddie followed Jane into the barn. When she

looked back, she saw Tibby sitting on the steps watching them.

Maddie and Angeline were planting flower seeds beside the front steps of Angeline's house. Tibby was playing in the field nearby.

"Looks like that old dog's taken up with her," Angeline said.

Maddie looked up. She could see the top of Jubal's head and the tip of his tail as he followed Tibby through the tall grass. Then she noticed Zebedee coming up the hill toward them.

"Reckon Daniel gave Zeb the afternoon off," Maddie said.

"We're nearly done here," Angeline said. "Why don't you go play with 'em?"

Maddie grinned and hugged her sister. Then she tore off across the field. Zebedee smiled and waved at her.

"Tibby!" Maddie called. "I'll race you and Zeb to the pond!"

The little girl's head jerked up. Then she bolted down the hill toward the pond, the dog barking furiously and running after her.

Maddie followed them, the grass slapping at her skirt as she ran.

"Hey! No fair!" Zebedee yelled. "Y'all got a head start!"

"You gonna stand there gripin' or you gonna run?" Maddie called over her shoulder.

"I'll show you runnin'," Zebedee hollered and took off after her.

Maddie made it to the pond just after Tibby. Collapsing in the grass beside the child, Maddie yelled to

Zebedee, "You call that runnin'? The *mules* could run faster'n that!"

When Zeb finally reached them, he was scowling and breathing hard. He fell to the ground beside Maddie. "Y'all don't play fair," he muttered.

Jubal loped over to Zebedee and began to lick his face.

"Stop that!" Zeb swatted playfully at the dog. "Get this critter off me." His tail beating the air, Jubal barked and leaped on Zebedee's chest.

Tibby watched it all in silence, but Maddie could see laughter in the child's eyes.

When the dog finally lay down to nap, Tibby ran to the pond and climbed onto a rock. She pulled her dress up to her knees and dangled her feet in the water. Maddie watched her, and Zebedee watched Maddie.

"You done good with her," he said.

Maddie's eyes were still on Tibby. "But I don't know what she's thinkin' or feelin'. Wish she'd talk to me."

"Right now I'd say she's feelin' happy," Zebedee said. "I knows I am. Seems like I been happy ever since I met you, Maddie Henry," he added in a quiet voice.

Maddie turned to look at Zeb, and his soft, dark eyes caught hers.

"Reckon it's time we talked," he said.

"Zeb, it's such a pretty day," Maddie said quickly. "Let's not be serious."

"But that's how I'm feelin'," he said softly. "How I been feelin' for a long time now. I wants to be part'a this family."

"You *are* part'a the family," Maddie said. "Mama thinks'a you as one of her own."

"What about you, Maddie? How do you think'a me?"

91

"You know I care about you," Maddie said. "Same as Angeline and Royall and everybody else does."

"Same as Angeline and Royall?" Zebedee asked. "Like I'm your brother, you mean."

"Like you're my brother and my best friend." Maddie knew the words would hurt him even as they came from her mouth. But they were the truth, and she didn't know what else to say.

"Oh." Zebedee looked down and started pulling at blades of grass.

"Zeb—"

"Don't say no more!" he said sharply. Then, "You're still set on goin' north, ain't you?"

"Yes," Maddie said, feeling miserable. "I've wanted it so long, I can't give it up."

He nodded, still not looking at her. "No, I reckon you can't," he said. "I knows what it's like to want somethin' real bad."

The sorrow and resignation in his voice cut into Maddie's heart. "Zeb, I'm sorry," she whispered.

"Nothin' to be sorry for," he said. "I just hope this dream'a yours makes you happy. But, Maddie, how *can* it make you happy if you don't have somebody to share it with?"

11

Maddie knew that Zebedee was going out of his way to avoid her. He left for the leather shop before breakfast and didn't come home until dark. In the evenings, when the rest of them gathered on the porch, Zeb walked the fields until bedtime. Pride and the dog usually went with him.

In August, when the corn began to grow tall, Zebedee started coming home in the afternoons to help with the weeding. But even then, he worked as far away from Maddie as possible. She realized that she had come to take Zebedee's friendship for granted. He had always been there to listen and comfort, to laugh and play. And now he was like a stranger. The hurt she felt was nearly more than Maddie could bear.

The fierce August sun was good for the growing corn but hard on the folks in the fields. Maddie put leaves in her bonnet to cool her head, but the heat still left her feeling limp and exhausted. By suppertime, it was all she could do to drag to the house and collapse on the porch.

When the weeding was finally done, Angeline and Royall went back to working on their house and Mama gave Maddie and Zebedee a day off. After morning chores were finished, Zebedee told Pride he'd take him fishing. Maddie was about to ask if she and Tibby could go along when Mama said, "I was gonna do the mendin' this mornin', but I'm outta thread. And we're gettin' low on cornmeal. Maddie, you reckon you could carry a sack'a meal back from town?"

Maddie watched in disappointment as Zebedee and Pride left the yard with their cane poles. "I can ride one'a the mules," she said.

Mama unpinned a little purse from her petticoat and started counting out coins. Then she paused and looked at Maddie.

"I don't know if you should go to Mister Gentry's store by yourself," Mama said. "Maybe you better wait till Zeb comes back."

Maddie was a little put out with Mama's worrying. After all, she wasn't a child, and she didn't need Zebedee to take care of her. Besides, the way he was feeling now, Zeb probably wouldn't want to go to town with her.

"He may not be back 'fore suppertime and you need the thread now," Maddie said. "Anyhow, Ruth goes to the store by herself all the time."

Mama hesitated, then handed the coins to Maddie. "All right, but if anybody gives you trouble, you come home quick."

"Yes'm," Maddie said. She was already climbing to the loft to change into her good dress.

"And Tibby's gonna need shoes when it gets cold," Mama called after her. "Stop by Daniel's on the way back and see if he'll make her some."

Maddie paused on the ladder and smiled. "I will, Mama. Thank you."

Tibby watched while Maddie put the bridle on the mule.

"You're gonna be gettin' new shoes," Maddie told her. "I 'spect you'll need to be there for Daniel to fit 'em." Then Maddie wondered if she should take Mama's fears more seriously. It was one thing for her to face a town of white folks, but taking a little girl along was something else again.

Tibby had climbed to the top fence rail. She was waiting patiently to be lifted onto the mule's back.

"You reckon you'll be scared in town?" Maddie asked her. "With all the folks around?"

Tibby frowned, considering. Then she shook her head and held out her arms for Maddie to lift her onto the mule.

With Tibby holding on to her waist, Maddie dug her heels into the old mule's sides and headed for the road. Mama's precious coins jingled in her skirt pocket.

Maddie thought about Zebedee as they rode toward town. She knew he was hurt and angry, but she couldn't believe he wouldn't get over it. With them living in the same house, he couldn't ignore her forever. She'd just have to make a point of being wherever he was and force him to talk to her. Then things could go back to being the way they used to be.

When Maddie passed the Loftis fields, she noticed that the corn was thick and leafy and higher than theirs. Folks were moving slowly up and down the rows with their hoes. In the next field, workers were picking beans. Mister Loftis and his son, Sam, were loading baskets of beans into a wagon.

The Loftis house and barns came into sight. With everybody working in the fields, the kitchen yard was deserted. But then Maddie saw two colored men coming down the steps from the back porch. She wondered what field workers were doing in Mister Loftis's house.

The men hurried across the kitchen yard and the barn lot. They climbed the fence to the pasture. When the smaller one jumped from the fence into the pasture, he turned toward Maddie. It was William! Ben and William sneaking off from work, Maddie thought. But what had they been doing in the house? She watched as they ran across the pasture, heading in the direction of town.

Maddie puzzled over what she had seen as the mule plodded down the road. She was sure Mister Loftis wouldn't want workers in his house, especially when he wasn't around. Had they gone in to steal from him? But Maddie didn't want to believe it. Ruth would be so disappointed in William. And Daniel would be furious. Could Mister Loftis have sent Ben to the house for something? Try as she might, Maddie couldn't come up with a reason for him to do that. And even if he had, why was William there? And why were they sneaking off through the pasture where nobody would see them?

Maddie wondered what she should do. If William was falling into bad habits because of Ben, shouldn't Ruth and Daniel be told? If somebody caught William stealing, there'd be big trouble. They'd send him to jail. Or worse. Maddie could picture the fury of men like Mister Gentry over a colored man stealing from a white man's house.

Maddie was still fretting over what she should do when she came to Daniel and Ruth's place. She thought about stopping and telling Ruth what she had seen, but she couldn't. If William hadn't done anything wrong, and Daniel accused him of stealing, it might pull the brothers apart forever.

As they entered town, Tibby's grasp tightened around Maddie's waist.

"It's all right," Maddie said. "You can wait outside the store for me. I'll just be a minute; then we'll go see about your shoes."

Maddie stopped the mule at the general store. Two white women in homespun dresses and cotton bonnets were standing out front. One of them was pointing down the street.

Maddie's eyes followed the woman's finger. She saw Jane Woods at the other end of the street, walking down the sidewalk with the blue parasol over her shoulder. Then Maddie became aware of what the women were saying.

"Just struttin' along like she owns the town," one woman said.

"Like she's white," the other added.

"Puttin' on airs with that fancy bonnet—and carryin' a parasol! Never seen anything like it in all my born days."

"What's them Nigras need with a teacher, anyhow? Just puttin' ideas in their heads, that's what." The woman's lips were pressed together in an angry line. "I do despise these Nigras. Yankees and Nigras—they done took it all!"

Maddie saw Jane go into a store that had bonnets in the window. The women walked away, still muttering as they moved down the sidewalk.

Maddie slid off the mule's back. Her hands were shaking as she tied the reins to the hitching post. The

97

women's words had hurt, but more than that, they had made Maddie angry. What had Jane ever done to them? What had any of the colored folks ever done to this town? If Jane wanted to carry a parasol and wear a pretty bonnet, she had every right to!

When Maddie looked up, her eyes met Tibby's. Tibby was clutching the mule's stiff mane and sitting very still.

Maddie came around to the side of the mule and pressed Tibby's clenched fists. She smiled. "I'll be right back. You sit here and wait for me. Will you do that?"

Tibby nodded.

"Good girl." Maddie patted Tibby's arm and went inside.

The store was cool and shadowy. Kerosene lamps cast a soft glow on the counters and the shelves, which rose from floor to ceiling. A blend of strong scents filled Maddie's nostrils: tobacco, molasses, and vinegar from the pickle barrel.

Maddie walked slowly down the center aisle. She stared in awe at all the fine goods: the bolts of calico and gingham in rainbow colors, the barrels of fish and salt pork and coffee, the tins of spices and tea and chocolate. Sacks of sugar and flour leaned against the wall. Fresh-baked bread and hoops of cheese covered a counter.

Then Maddie saw the dolls. Five of them were lined up on one of the high shelves. She had never seen such beautiful dolls. They weren't sewn from rags like the ones Mama had stitched for her and Angeline. Their faces looked real, with soft, pink cheeks and blue eyes and tiny pearl teeth showing through rose-colored smiles. And their hair wasn't made from yarn; it was gold and shiny like Mistress McCartha's, tied back with ribbons or peeking out from under velvet bonnets.

Maddie stared at the dolls, taking in every detail of their finery and thinking how Tibby would love them. For a moment, she thought about bringing Tibby in to see the dolls, but then she saw Mister Gentry. He was in the back of the store, reaching for items on a shelf as a white woman checked them off her list.

Maddie felt a twinge of fear at the sight of the man. Forgetting about the dolls, she walked to where sacks of cornmeal were stacked against the wall. She picked up one of the heavy sacks and went in search of thread.

Spools of thread in every color were displayed with scissors, thimbles, and pretty buttons. But they were behind glass, and Maddie realized she'd have to ask for Mama's thread. She stood at the counter and waited for Mister Gentry to finish helping the woman. When they finally came to the front of the store, he was carrying the woman's basket and telling her about the new printed calico he'd just gotten in. He brushed past Maddie without seeming to notice her.

Maddie followed him and the woman to the front counter. She waited while Mister Gentry added up the purchases and took the woman's money. When the woman headed for the door, Maddie stepped up to the counter.

Mister Gentry had been smiling at the white woman. He didn't smile at Maddie. "What you want?" he asked, barely looking at her.

"This cornmeal," Maddie said, laying the sack on the counter. "And a spool'a white thread."

The storekeeper glanced at the sack of meal. Then he picked up a cloth and began to rub it on the counter glass, like he was wiping off a spot of dirt. Only the glass looked clean to Maddie. He took his time rubbing; then he folded the cloth and put it back under the counter. When he looked up again, his eyes slid past her. He was staring over her shoulder, frowning.

Maddie turned around and saw William and Ben come in. William stopped dead still when he saw Maddie, but Ben just grinned and pulled William into the store.

"How do, Miz Maddie," Ben said in his sassy way. He sidled up to the counter and bent down to look at the pocket knives behind the glass.

"Hello," Maddie said. She was looking at William, but he wouldn't meet her eyes.

"What you boys doin' in here?" Mister Gentry asked sharply.

"I's thinkin' on gettin' me one'a these here knives," Ben said.

"They don't come free," the storekeeper said.

Ben's grin faltered, then steadied. "Didn't figger they did," he said easily. "My friend's got money. Gonna buy me a present, ain't you, Will?"

William nodded, but he didn't look up from the floor.

"I like the looks'a that one with the black carved handle," Ben said. "Pretty, ain't it?"

Mister Gentry's face tightened. "That's the most expensive one I got," he said.

"How much?" Ben asked.

"More'n you have," Mister Gentry said. "So you boys move along; quit wastin' my time."

Ben was staring hard at the man. "I told you my friend's got money. Show him, Will."

When William didn't move, Ben grabbed his arm. "Show him the money."

William dug into his pocket and withdrew a fist. When he opened his hand, Maddie saw four quarters on his palm. She felt sick, certain now that they had stolen the money from Mister Loftis.

"Where'd you get this money, boy?" Mister Gentry demanded.

"His brother give it to him," Ben said. He wasn't grinning anymore. "How much for the knife?"

"It's already sold," Mister Gentry said in a cold voice. "They're all sold. Now you boys get outta my store 'fore I set the sheriff on you."

Ben looked like he was getting ready to argue when William said, "I'm goin'," and headed for the door. Ben glanced at Maddie, his eyes filled with anger, as he followed William out of the store.

Mister Gentry muttered something under his breath. Then he looked at Maddie. "You gonna tell me what else you need?" he asked sharply.

"A spool'a white thread," she said.

The man got the thread and slapped it down on the counter next to the cornmeal. When he told her how much she owed, Maddie reached for the coins in her pocket. She was so nervous and upset about William, she dropped some pennies on the floor.

"Pick 'em up," the storekeeper barked at her. "I don't have all day."

Maddie paid him and hurried out of the store. Tibby was still waiting where Maddie had left her.

"You're a good girl," Maddie said as she jumped on the mule's back and picked up the reins.

Maddie noticed a few people watching them as they

rode through town. She heard a man say something about "that little yaller gal" and then he laughed. Maddie dug her heels into the mule's sides and urged him on as fast as his legs would go.

She knew she had to say something to Ruth and Daniel about William before Mister Loftis realized his money was missing. Maybe Ben had been telling the truth about Daniel giving him the money, but Maddie doubted it.

She found Daniel in the leather shop with Zebedee. "I need to talk to you and Ruth about William," she said to Daniel.

"You better tell me first," Daniel said. He sounded tired. "You can talk in front'a Zeb."

As Maddie told him what she had seen, Daniel looked stunned. When she was finished, he shook his head. "I didn't give him the money," he said.

"Maybe he got it from somebody else," Maddie said quickly. "Maybe he earned it."

"Doin' what?" Daniel asked. "He don't even do his share around here. Zeb can tell you that."

Zebedee came over to where Daniel was sitting. "You need to talk to William 'fore you think the worst," Zebedee said.

Daniel nodded. He still didn't look angry, as Maddie had feared he would be. But the hurt look in his eyes was worse than anger, she thought.

"They could hang him," Daniel muttered. Suddenly he stood up and reached for his hat. "You see which way he went?" Daniel asked Maddie.

Maddie shook her head. "I'm sorry I had to tell you," she said.

Daniel touched her arm. "No, Maddie. I thank you

102

for tellin' me. I gotta do somethin' to help that boy. Lord knows I never wuz around when he needed me. I can't let him down this time."

When Daniel was gone, Maddie turned to Zebedee. She half expected him to walk away, but instead, he wrapped his arms around her and pulled her close.

"You done the right thing, Maddie Henry," he said softly.

And Maddie began to cry.

12

Late that afternoon, Ruth knocked on the door and stuck her head in. Maddie leaped up from the table, and the beans she was breaking spilled all over the floor. Mama stooped down to pick them up without saying a word.

"Did Daniel find him?" Maddie asked quickly.

Ruth nodded.

"Child, you look plumb give out," Mama said to Ruth. "Sit yourself down and I'll pour you a cup'a cold milk."

Ruth sank into Mama's rocker. She did look hot and tired.

"William all right?" Maddie asked.

"He's at the shop with Daniel and Zeb," Ruth said. She reached for the cup Mama had brought her. "Thank you, Miz Ella." Ruth took a sip of milk and leaned back in the chair. "Daniel found 'em down at the river drinkin' whiskey. Daniel said when he asked William if he stole the money from Mister Loftis, William owned up to it right off and started cryin'. Ben tried to hush him up, but William told Daniel ever'thing."

"Sounds like Ben was behind it all," Maddie said.

"But William went along with it," Ruth said. "Ben was in the kitchen yard this mornin' when a man wuz makin' the payment on some hogs he bought from Mister Loftis. Ben seen the Loftis boy take the money and leave it on the table in the kitchen. When ever'body went to the fields, Ben run and got William and they took the money."

"Sam's gonna remember he left the money on the table," Maddie said.

"Daniel took William and Ben back to the Loftis house and made 'em put it back," Ruth said. "Mister Loftis and Sam wuz still in the fields."

Maddie sighed with relief. "Then ever'thing's all right."

Ruth looked troubled. "But William still took the money. Daniel's frettin' over whether he done the right thing—lettin' the boys get off scot-free like that. He tore into 'em somethin' fierce—told 'em iffen he ever heared about 'em stealin' again, he'd turn 'em over to the sheriff hisself. And he made it clear William couldn't have nothin' more to do with Ben. William can't leave our place without Daniel or me with him."

"You think William's learned a lesson?" Mama asked.

"I don't know, Miz Ella," Ruth said. "He wuz still cryin' and sayin' how sorry he wuz when Daniel brung him home—but he got mad when Daniel told him he couldn't see Ben no more." Ruth sighed. "Sez Ben used to look out for him after me and Daniel wuz gone. William sez Ben stole food from the storehouse so's they wouldn't starve."

That night, Maddie lay awake a long time. Tibby had left her mattress and was curled up against Maddie's back. On the other side of the thin wall, Maddie could hear Pride mumbling in his sleep. She wondered if

Zebedee was asleep or if he was staring into the darkness as she was.

Maddie thought about how it had felt when Zeb put his arms around her that morning. All the times they had hugged each other, and she'd never noticed before how strong he was. Strong, but gentle. Like Papa.

She heard Zeb saying, "You done the right thing, Maddie Henry," and tears filled her eyes. Maddie Henry. The way Zeb said it, you'd have thought it was the most beautiful name in the world.

She remembered when they were younger, running through the woods on the island, catching shad in the sound. Zebedee had always been there, teasing, caring, making her believe she could do anything.

And this morning he had been there for her again. He'd seen her doubts and fears, as he always did, and pushed aside his own hurt feelings to comfort her. How could she have taken that sweet caring for granted? Maddie felt a raw pain inside, thinking how unfeeling she must have seemed to Zeb. But it wasn't too late. She could still make it up to him. She'd tell him that she understood now. That he was right—there was nothing more important than being there for the folks you love.

Maddie came downstairs before the sun was up, but Zebedee had already left for work. She swallowed her disappointment and started fixing breakfast. When she called Pride and Tibby in to eat, Jubal ran in with them.

Mama was carrying a pan of biscuits to the table. The dog leaped up on her, slobbering happily on her apron and sniffing at the hot, buttery biscuits.

Mama yanked the pan back and glared at the animal. "Get down, you varmint! What's this critter doin' in my house? Out! Get outta my house!"

Jubal sat down at Mama's feet and cocked his head, his eyes still on the biscuits, his tail thumping the floorboards.

Mama placed the biscuits on the table. She turned to Pride and Tibby, hands on her hips. "What you mean bringin' that dog in here? Mud all over him. And on my clean floor."

Pride and Tibby exchanged a look. Pride was trying to keep a straight face, but a grin was tugging at his lips. Tibby ducked her head, but not before Maddie saw her smile. Then Tibby began to giggle.

Mama and Maddie stared at Tibby in surprise. Mama's hands dropped to her sides.

"Well, don't just stand there," Mama said gruffly. "Sit down 'fore the food's stone cold. And right after break-fast, Mister Pride and Miz Tibby can mop the floor. Don't wanta see a speck'a dirt left."

Tibby squeezed onto the bench next to Maddie. Mama didn't say a word when Tibby slipped Jubal a biscuit.

Maddie tried to catch Zebedee alone all week, but he was still putting in long hours at the leather shop. When he was home, everybody else was there and Mad-die felt shy about asking to talk to him alone. At least he seemed to have gotten over being mad at her, Mad-die thought with relief. Whenever she saw him, he'd grin and act like nothing had changed. So Maddie decided to wait a while to talk to him. One of these days, they'd find themselves alone and she could tell him how she felt.

It was the end of August and the corn was growing tall. They were all in the fields again, weeding the corn and the vegetables. Royall was so excited, he didn't even seem to mind the long days in the sun.

"Miz Ella, we got a fine corn crop," he said happily. "A month from now, we's gonna be makin' some money."

"Then we oughta celebrate," Mama said. "This week after services, we'll have Daniel and Ruth and the Spiveys over for dinner. And William, too, if he'll come. And we'll ask Brother Isaac and Jane. I got squash and peas comin' in, and I'll fry up some chicken."

After church that Sunday, Royall and Zebedee set up a table in the yard using barrels and wide boards. Mama covered the boards with her best quilt. Soon the guests started arriving, bringing pies and cakes and covered dishes.

When Brother Isaac's wagon pulled in, Jane was sitting beside him. Maddie ran out to meet them.

Jane stepped down from the wagon seat, balancing her parasol in one hand and a loaf of freshly baked bread in the other. She handed the bread to Maddie and reached into the wagon for a book.

"You said you hadn't read anything by Mister Charles Dickens," Jane said. "I think you'll like this one. It's called *A Tale of Two Cities.*"

Mama came out and hugged Jane. "That bread sure smells good," she said. "Brother Isaac, come on and sit yourself down. Dinner's just about ready."

Ruth and Jane helped Maddie carry the food to the table. After Brother Isaac said grace, Mama urged everybody to dig in.

"Miz Ella, this chicken is mighty good," Brother Isaac said. "Mighty good."

"And these wonderful apple dumplings," Jane said.

William was sitting at the end of the table, staring at his plate. He hadn't said a word since he got there. Maddie passed him a plate of corn bread.

"You better grab yourself a second piece while you're at it," Maddie said. "Else Royall and Pride'll take it all."

William glanced at Maddie, looking shy and ill at ease. Maddie's heart softened a little toward him.

"And try some apple butter on it," Maddie said. "Mama makes the best apple butter."

William filled his plate as Maddie passed him platters and bowls. He nodded when he tasted the apple butter. "It's real good," he said softly.

"I see you brought Maddie another book," Angeline said to Jane. "I swear, that child would rather read than eat."

Maddie chewed and swallowed. "You wouldn't know it to see me now, would you?"

Zebedee smiled at her from across the table. "Reckon eatin' and readin's about the same to you, Maddie—you need one as much as the other."

Maddie felt a warm glow spread over her. She knew now that Zebedee had forgiven her. After dinner, when everybody had gone home, she'd tell him how wrong she'd been. Everything was going to be all right now.

"Maddie was tellin' me about one book you loaned her," Angeline said to Jane. "The one about the governess that's engaged to the plantation owner's son, and then they find out she's the daughter of a slave."

Jane nodded. "That book's ahead of its time. At first we think Herbert, the son, will follow the traditional path. He breaks off his engagement to Helen, as he's expected to, and Helen leaves the plantation for Italy."

"But then Herbert learns he can't be happy without her," Maddie said. "He follows her to Italy and they get married."

"The author couldn't very well let them stay in this country," Jane said. "There's no place here where a white man and a colored woman would be allowed to marry."

"Not even Ohio?" Maddie asked.

Jane shook her head. "Not even Ohio."

There was silence for a moment. Then Royall said, "But we's free now. We got a lot to be thankful for."

"We surely do," Daniel said. He looked at Ruth and smiled. "I reckon this is a good time to share Ruth and Zeb's good news with y'all."

Maddie felt a sudden chill. She looked quickly at Ruth, who was beaming, and then at Zebedee, who was smiling shyly at Ruth.

"Zebedee come to me yesterday and asked if he could marry my sister," Daniel said. "And seein' as how that's what she wants, I gave 'em my blessin'."

For an instant, it seemed to Maddie that nobody breathed. Then they were all talking at once.

"Congratulations, Zebedee," Jane said. "Ruth's a fine young woman."

"You old dog!" Royall slapped Zebedee on the back. "And you never even let on."

"Ruth, I'm happy for you," Angeline said.

Everybody was smiling and moving and offering their congratulations. Everybody except Maddie. The voices and bodies whirled around her in a jumble of sound and color. She wondered why she was feeling so dizzy. And why she couldn't make any words come out of her mouth.

Then Ruth was beside her. The girl's happy face swam before Maddie's eyes, then steadied.

"Zeb just asked me yesterday," Ruth was saying. "I nearly told you at services this mornin' but we'd decided to tell ever'body at one time. Maddie, I'm so happy I could bust. Now we'll be almost like sisters."

Maddie felt herself smile at Ruth. "It's wonderful," she heard herself saying. "Zeb is so dear to us—you're both so dear." Then she was hugging Ruth.

Over Ruth's shoulder, Maddie saw Zebedee watching them. He looks happy, Maddie thought. But the eyes that met hers seemed to be asking for something.

Maddie pulled away slowly from Ruth and reached for her hand. She led Ruth to where Zebedee waited. "I'm glad for both'a you," Maddie said, looking at Zeb. "I know you'll be happy. You deserve to be happy."

The question in Zebedee's eyes had faded away. He smiled at her, that tender, familiar smile, and then his arms were around her.

"So do you, Maddie Henry," Zeb whispered.

Maddie was drying the last of the dishes when Mama came into the storeroom carrying the quilt she'd used for a tablecloth. Mama folded the quilt carefully, not looking at Maddie. Finally, she said, "You didn't know about Zeb and Ruth?"

"Not till Daniel told us." Maddie began to stack plates on the shelf.

"I always figgered it'd be you and Zeb," Mama said.

111

"Ruth loves him."

"I can see she does," Mama said. "It's not Ruth's feelin's I wonder about."

Maddie turned to face Mama. "I'd been thinkin' lately that maybe Zeb and I should be together," she said. "But I waited too long."

Mama's eyes grew moist. She held out her arms and Maddie ran into them. Mama stood there rocking her gently.

"Ruth'll be a good wife," Maddie said as her tears began to fall on Mama's shoulder. "And Zeb's happy. I want him to be happy, Mama. I do!"

"I know you do, sugar babe," Mama said. "I know you do."

13

In September, the corn was ready to be picked. Zebedee drove the wagon to the field, and they threw the ripe ears into the wagon bed. After supper each night, they went to the barn and shucked corn by lantern light until bedtime. Royall had been right. They had a good crop, even with the late planting.

"We're gonna be able to buy you that window glass, Miz Ella," Royall said.

"I'm makin' a list of ever'thing we need," Mama said. And Maddie could tell that Mama was happy.

The morning Royall and Zebedee left to take the corn to market, Mama was canning beans from her garden, and Pride and Tibby were picking apples. Maddie and Angeline were in the field digging up sweet potatoes.

Angeline sat down between the rows and wiped her face. "Reckon Zeb won't be with us much longer," she said. "Ruth says they'll be buildin' a house back'a Daniel's."

"Ruth told me."

"Maddie, you haven't said how you feel about Ruth and Zebedee gettin' married."

"I love 'em both," Maddie said softly. Then she looked down at Angeline and grinned. "Now don't go frettin' over me. I'm glad for Ruth and Zeb. I'll dance and sing at their weddin'."

Maddie went back to work, even humming a little to show Angeline how really fine she was. But that lonesome feeling was still there. It had crept into her heart and made a hollow place that nothing seemed to fill.

Royall poured the money on the table. Pride looked at it with wide eyes. "Are we rich?" he asked.

"Not hardly," Royall said, smiling. "But I reckon we got all we need."

Mama pulled out her list. "Maddie, can you and Zeb handle all this?" she asked.

"And me," Pride said. "I wanta go to town, too."

Zebedee grinned. "You gonna behave yourself if we take you?"

Pride whooped. He was already running out the door.

"Come back here!" Mama yelled. "You gotta change your clothes to go to town." She looked at Maddie's muddy dress. "All'a you gotta clean up."

After Maddie had washed her hands and face, she went to the loft to change clothes. She found Tibby pulling the pink and brown dress over her head.

Maddie smiled. "Reckon there's no way we're leavin' you behind," she said. "All right, bring me the comb so's I can fix your hair."

Pride stood behind the wagon seat, holding on to Zebedee's shoulders and chattering all the way to town. Maddie was grateful. She hadn't been alone with Zeb since Daniel announced the wedding plans, and she wasn't sure what to say to him.

Tibby sat in Maddie's lap, looking at everything they passed with curious eyes.

"She still ain't said nothin'?" Zeb asked during a brief silence.

"No, but she's real smart," Maddie said. "She follows along in the books at school, and I swear she knows some'a the words already."

Zebedee nodded. "Reckon it couldn't be no other way with you for a mama."

Mama? Maddie looked down at the top of Tibby's head and then at Zeb. He was grinning at the look on her face. "Her mama," he said again.

Zebedee stopped the wagon in front of the store. Pride leaped to the ground.

"Now, you wait," Maddie said to him. "You and Tibby gotta stay with me."

"Then come on," Pride said impatiently. "I never been to a store before. I wanta see what they got."

Mister Gentry was at the front counter talking to two men. Maddie took Pride and Tibby's hands and hurried past without looking at him. Dewey Gentry was taking brown glass bottles from a carton and lining them up on a shelf. Maddie read *Prof. Low's Liniment and Worm Syrup* on one of the bottles.

Zebedee went to the back of the store to look at tools. Royall had told him to price claw hammers and mattocks. Maddie pulled out Mama's list.

"Look, Maddie." Pride was pointing at a box of tiny soldiers in Confederate-gray uniforms. Some were on horseback, and one carried the flag of the Confederacy.

"You can look, but don't touch anything," Maddie warned him. Then she noticed Tibby staring in awe at the dolls. She had been right to guess that Tibby would love them.

Maddie placed a hand on Pride's shoulder and one

115

on Tibby's. "You stay here and look at the pretties while I get the things on Mama's list. Don't go anywhere else, all right?"

Pride nodded, but Tibby didn't seem to have heard her. She was still gazing at the dolls with soft, amazed eyes.

"Pride, you watch after Tibby," Maddie said. She looked at Mama's list.

> Salt, 1 pound
> Coffee, 3 pounds
> Sugar, 2 pounds
> Molasses, 1 gallon
> Salted herring, 2 dozen
> Cheese, 1 pound
> Quilting needle
> Black thread
> Cotton flannel, 3 yards

Maddie smiled at the next entry.

> Calico (dress for Maddie & 1 for Tibby)

But then Maddie realized with dismay that she would have to ask Mister Gentry for every item on the list. She glanced at the front counter. He was still talking to the two men.

Maddie sighed. Well, there was no way around it. She walked slowly to the front of the store.

One of the men was leaning on the counter and talking loud. "—and they's votin' to outlaw slavery in North Carolina," he was saying.

"Thought the Yankees already done that," the other man grumbled. "Why's the state convention have to do it all over?"

116

Mister Gentry looked angry. " 'Cause the Yankees wanta rub our noses in it, that's why. And make it look like we're doin' it on our own."

"I heared there's gonna be niggers at the convention," one of the men said. "They's sayin' they oughta be able to hold public office and testify in court. You ever heared'a such nonsense?"

"Hold public office? They do good to know their own names," Mister Gentry said.

"We can't have niggers givin' evidence in court." The man grabbed his package off the counter. "I'd like to go to that convention myself—tell 'em what's what."

The other man snickered. "They don't wanta hear from you, Lester. Your skin ain't dark enough."

The two men started for the door, still talking.

"You boys come back," Mister Gentry called after them.

Maddie had been standing close enough to hear everything the men said. She didn't know what the state convention was, but it sounded like colored folks were being given a chance to speak up for themselves. No wonder Mister Gentry and his friends were mad.

Maddie didn't know whether to be happy about what she had heard or sorry she was here when the storekeeper was in such a bad mood. But she had to get the things on Mama's list. Maddie moved to the counter and held out the paper to Mister Gentry.

He looked at the list, then at Maddie. When he didn't respond, Maddie said, "I need the things written on this paper, please."

The man snatched the list from her and studied it, frowning. Finally, he said, "You got money to pay for all this? I don't give credit to coloreds."

"I can pay," Maddie said, trying to sound firm but polite.

Mister Gentry grunted, looking like he'd rather go broke than sell goods to Maddie. But he went over to a barrel and started scooping coffee into a sack. When the sack was full, he moved to the sugar barrel and began to fill another sack.

When Zebedee came to the front of the store with Tibby and Pride, the counter was stacked high with Maddie's purchases. Mister Gentry was adding up what she owed.

"Herring, penny apiece, that's twenty-four cents," the man muttered as he wrote on a slip of paper. "Molasses, seventy cents; cheese, sixty cents; coffee—three pounds at fifty cents a pound . . ."

Zebedee was watching the man. He glanced at the list on the counter, looking puzzled.

"That'll be twelve dollars and thirty-four cents," Mister Gentry said.

Maddie began to count out the money.

" 'Scuse me, sir," Zebedee said, and Maddie turned to stare at him. "I think there's a mistake."

Mister Gentry frowned. "What kinda mistake?"

"That cheese is marked thirty cents a pound, but you charged us sixty cents," Zebedee said.

"I did no such thing!" The color was rising in the storekeeper's face.

"I believe you did, sir," Zebedee said in a quiet voice. "Reckon you thought we'd bought two pounds."

"You callin' me a liar, boy?"

"No, sir," Zebedee said softly. "It wuz just a mistake, I reckon. If you look at your figgers—"

"No need to look," Mister Gentry said sharply. "I figgered right. And I don't take kindly to you questionin' my honesty!"

Dewey Gentry had come to the front of the store. "This boy givin' you trouble, Pa? Want me to teach him to mind his manners?"

"Zeb, it's all right," Maddie said quickly. She handed Mister Gentry the money. He grabbed it from her and began to count.

"He overcharged you," Zebedee said to Maddie.

"Let's go," Maddie said in an urgent voice. She started gathering up packages from the counter.

"What you mean callin' my pa a liar?" Dewey demanded.

"Didn't call nobody a liar," Zebedee said. Maddie was pulling on his arm, but he didn't move.

"Zeb, the children," she whispered.

Zebedee glanced down at Pride and Tibby. They were watching him with wide eyes. Tibby was hanging on to Maddie's skirt.

Maddie placed the sacks of coffee and sugar into Zebedee's arms. "Come on, Zeb," she said. "We gotta be gettin' home."

Zebedee looked from Dewey's angry face to Maddie's frightened one. He nodded abruptly and reached for the jug of molasses. Dewey grabbed his wrist.

"I've had a bellyful'a you and your kind," Dewey said, his eyes bright with fury. "You come in here and 'spect us to wait on you like you wuz somebody, and you ain't nobody. Just a dumb nigger."

Zebedee's body grew rigid. He jerked his arm from Dewey's grasp.

119

For an instant, Maddie feared that Zeb was going to hit Dewey. Then Mister Gentry came out from behind the counter.

"Get outta my store," the man said to Zebedee. His voice was icy. "And don't come back."

Maddie grabbed the fabric from the counter and reached for Tibby's hand. Zebedee picked up the jug of molasses and followed Maddie and the children to the door.

"If there's trouble, I'll know who caused it!" Mister Gentry called after him. "And I'll know where to come lookin' for you!"

14

"Y'all ready to leave?" Royall called from the porch.

"Just about," Maddie answered. She looked at Tibby. "Turn around so I can get a good look at you."

Tibby was wearing the blue calico dress Mama had made for her. She was also wearing new high-topped shoes.

Tibby turned around slowly, frowning at her feet.

"You're a picture," Maddie said. "And you'll get used to the shoes."

Tibby looked doubtful.

Mama came rushing out of the storeroom carrying a basket of food. "We best hurry," she said. "Can't be late for Zeb's weddin'." She stopped to look at Tibby. "My, if you're not a pretty one," she said, and Tibby smiled.

Pride was already in the wagon with Angeline and Elizabeth. Royall took Mama's basket and put it in the wagon next to the food Angeline was taking.

"You reckon this'll be enough?" Mama fretted as Royall helped her into the wagon. "I shoulda brought more squash."

"There's food to feed us a solid week," Royall said. He clucked to the mules, and they started down the road.

Maddie spread out the skirt of her dress so it wouldn't wrinkle. She smoothed her hair. Then she smiled to herself. Anybody would think *she* was the bride, the way she was fussing. But Ruth was the one marrying Zebedee, and after today, nothing would be the same. The little house behind Daniel's was finished, and Zebedee would be living there now with his wife.

Zeb married. Maddie still wasn't used to the idea, but she was determined that today would be a joyous one for Ruth and Zebedee. Nothing was going to cast a shadow over their wedding, least of all the feelings of sadness that came over Maddie whenever she thought about losing Zeb.

All the workers from the Loftis farm were gathered around makeshift tables in the churchyard when Royall pulled the wagon to a stop. Ruth and Zebedee were standing near the church door with Daniel and William. Ruth was wearing a pale yellow dress and holding a bouquet of yellow partridge peas and ox-eye daisies.

Maddie climbed down from the wagon and hurried over to Ruth.

"Maddie, thank goodness you're here," Ruth said in a breathless voice. "I thought you wasn't comin'."

"You think I'd miss your weddin'?" Maddie demanded.

"Wouldn't of been no weddin' if you hadn't come," Zebedee said. "Ruth wuz ready to call the whole thing off."

He was teasing, of course. When Maddie saw the way Ruth looked at Zebedee, she knew that nothing would keep Ruth from marrying him.

Folks were starting to go inside. Brother Isaac came over to Ruth and Zebedee.

"You ready to become man and wife?" he asked, beaming at them.

Maddie saw Zebedee squeeze Ruth's hand. Then he took Maddie's hand and pressed it just as hard. "We's all gonna be family now," he said.

Maddie nodded. She could still feel the warmth from his hand as she followed Zeb and Ruth into the church.

Later, folks would say there was a special glow in the church that day. It could have been the sunlight streaming through loose boards; but the light seemed to focus at the front of the church where Ruth and Zebedee stood side-by-side before Brother Isaac, their faces radiant and expectant.

Sitting between Mama and Tibby, Maddie never took her eyes from the couple. When Brother Isaac asked Zebedee, "Do you take this woman to be your wife?" Maddie could hear the joy and certainty in Zeb's voice as he answered, "I do." When the preacher asked Ruth if she would take Zebedee to be her husband, Ruth turned to Zebedee and smiled tenderly at him before saying, "I do."

Then Brother Isaac read a verse from the Bible that brought tears to the eyes of many in the congregation.

> *Live joyfully with the wife whom thou lovest all the days of the life of thy vanity, which He hath given thee under the sun, all the days of thy vanity; for that is thy portion in this life, and in thy labor which thou takest under the sun.*

Zebedee was truly happy. Maddie knew that now. And she also knew that if ever there were two people who would live joyfully together all their days, those people were Ruth and Zebedee.

Maddie sat in the grass watching the dancing. Some of the men had brought fiddles and drums, and their music filled the warm autumn air. Angeline and Royall whirled past, then Ruth and Zebedee. Tibby stood next to Maddie, swaying in time to the music.

"Come on," Maddie said suddenly. She jumped up and grabbed Tibby's hands.

At first, Tibby just stood there, looking puzzled as Maddie began to move her feet and swing Tibby's arms.

"See, you step like this," Maddie said.

Tibby watched Maddie's feet. Then, tentatively, she began to move her own.

Maddie sang the words she remembered from plantation days.

Jimmy crack corn and I don't care,
Jimmy crack corn and I don't care,
Jimmy crack corn and I don't care,
My master's gone away!

Tibby laughed as Maddie whirled her around, and Maddie laughed with her.

With Zebedee gone, the house seemed empty. Maddie spent more time with Pride and Tibby, taking them fishing or into the woods to pick sweet persimmons and chinkapins. Sometimes Jane went with them.

The children had come to love Jane. She told them wonderful stories about kings and queens, warriors, and witches.

One day Maddie and Jane sat by the pond watching Pride and Tibby skip stones across the water.

"You seem restless," Jane said after a while.

"Reckon I am a little," Maddie said. She lay back in the grass and looked up at the cloudless sky. "Tell me about Ohio. What's it like?"

"Well, some of it doesn't look much different than here," Jane said. "We have farms and fields and ponds. But we have big cities, too. With tall buildings and lots of people living close together. And the streets are filled with carriages and people selling fish and charcoal and hot corn." Jane studied Maddie's face. "You want to go north, don't you?"

Maddie nodded. "But I don't have the money. Mama needs every cent we made from the crops."

"Are you sure you're ready to leave your family?" Jane asked. "They seem to depend on you."

"I don't want to leave then," Maddie said softly. "But I've never been anywhere. I want to see the big cities. And maybe," she added shyly, "maybe I could go to college someday, like you. That probably sounds silly," she went on quickly, "a slave girl thinkin' she's smart enough to go to college."

"No," Jane said firmly, "it doesn't sound silly at all. You're bright, Maddie. You can do anything you put your mind to."

"But it costs money," Maddie said. "Maybe I could get some kinda work up North, but I gotta earn the fare to get there."

"I think I know how you can earn some money," Jane said.

Maddie sat up quickly. "You do? How?"

125

"Emma Hawkins lives in the cabin next to mine," Jane said. "She used to keep house for a white woman in town—a Miz Colegrove. Emma's too old to do that kind of work anymore and she had to quit. She said Miz Colegrove was upset because she couldn't find anyone to work for her."

"How much does it pay?"

"She paid Emma a dollar a week."

Maddie smiled. A dollar a week. If she gave Mama half what she made, she could still save two dollars a month. Surely she'd have enough to pay her fare north by spring—or summer at the latest.

"Where does this Miz Colegrove live?" Maddie asked.

"Totin' and fetchin' for a white woman?" Angeline stood in the middle of the front room with her hands on her hips. "Maddie, are you outta your head?"

Maddie reached for her shawl. "Maybe. But I'm still gonna see if the job's been filled."

Mama was stirring a pot of stew over the fire. "We don't need the money."

"I need my own money," Maddie said. "I'll give you half, Mama."

"I said we don't need it," Mama said sharply. "Why you wanta go work for some white woman now you're free?"

"Like you're still a slave," Angeline added.

"Slaves didn't get paid a dollar a week," Maddie said. She put on her bonnet and tied it under her chin. "I'll be back 'fore long, Mama."

As she and Tibby walked down the road toward town, Maddie tried not to think about what Mama and Angeline had said. She didn't really want to keep house for a white woman, but how else could she make that much money? And with Zebedee gone, Maddie was more anxious than ever to get on with her life.

Mama and Angeline and Pride were doing fine, Maddie assured herself. They had Royall to care for them. They had a home and good friends. There was no reason now for Maddie to stay. Except— Her eyes fell on Tibby, who was skipping happily down the road ahead, not realizing that her small world was about to change forever.

Maddie felt a pang of guilt. She had opened her arms and her heart to the little girl, and Tibby had bravely rushed in. How hurt she would be if Maddie left her! But it wasn't as though she was leaving tomorrow, Maddie reasoned. Over the next few months, she would pull back slowly, allowing Tibby to depend on her less and less. After a while, Maddie figured, Tibby would rely more on Mama and Angeline and the others.

As Maddie silently planned all this, Tibby suddenly looked back at her and smiled. Maddie wasn't prepared for how that sweet, open smile would tug at her heart.

A dozen houses lined the narrow street behind the blacksmith's shop. The Colegrove house was at the end of the street, sitting like a fat white hen in the shade of old magnolia trees. The iron gate creaked when Maddie opened it. Tibby followed Maddie hesitantly down the stone walk and around the house. She waited in the yard while Maddie climbed the steps to the back door and knocked.

The door was opened by a tiny woman in a black dress. Her face was no bigger than Tibby's, Maddie

127

thought, but it was lined and spotted with age. The hair pulled back tightly into a knot at her neck was pure white.

"Miz Colegrove?" Maddie moved closer to the door and the woman stepped back.

"You got my name right," the woman said. She looked suspicious. "If you're here to sell somethin'—"

"No, ma'am," Maddie said quickly. "My name's Maddie Henry. I've come to ask if you've found somebody to keep house for you. 'Cause if you haven't, I'd like the job."

The woman peered at Maddie, her dark eyes nearly disappearing into folds of wrinkled skin. "Who sent you?"

"A friend'a Emma Hawkins," Maddie said. "My family just moved to Willoughby last spring. We live out past Mister Loftis's place—"

"Don't need to hear your whole life story," the woman snapped. "Can you clean a house?"

"Yes, ma'am."

"And do wash? And iron? I won't put up with sloppy work. Took me two years to teach Emma how to press a petticoat to my likin'."

"Yes, ma'am," Maddie repeated.

"Whad you say your name was?"

"Maddie Hen—"

"Don't need your last name," Miz Colegrove interrupted her. "Won't be sendin' you no invitations to supper. Be here at seven in the mornin'."

"Yes, ma'am. Thank you, ma'am."

"I'll want you here at seven ever' mornin', Monday through Friday," the woman went on. "If you finish your work, you can leave at noon. We'll talk pay when I

128

see if you know how to do anything." She looked at Tibby for the first time and stared hard at her for a moment. "And leave the little picaninny home. You won't have time to tend her."

Before Maddie could respond, the door closed in her face.

15

After breakfast, Maddie set out for Miz Colegrove's house. When Tibby ran down the steps after her, Maddie stopped.

"You can't come with me today," Maddie said. "Go back inside and help Mama put the dishes away."

Tibby continued across the yard.

"Tibby, you hear me?" Maddie asked in a firm voice. "I'm goin' to work. You gotta stay home."

Tibby passed Maddie without looking at her and started down the road. Maddie hurried to catch up with the child. She grabbed Tibby's arm.

"Come on," Maddie said. "I'm takin' you home."

Tibby pouted and tried to pull free all the way back to the house. When they reached the porch steps, Tibby grabbed on to the railing and refused to go up the steps.

"I don't have time for this foolishness," Maddie said. "Let go, Tibby."

Mama came out on the porch. "What's goin' on?"

"I can't take Tibby," Maddie said. "Will you hold her till I'm gone?"

"You can help me in the garden," Mama said as she wrapped her arms around the child.

Maddie bent down and stroked Tibby's face. "Be a good girl till I get back."

Tibby glared at her and hugged the railing more tightly.

"Thank you, Mama," Maddie said. She gave Tibby a hasty pat on the arm and hurried down the steps. She was halfway across the yard when she heard Tibby start to cry. Then wail. The sound wrenched at Maddie's heart, but she refused to turn around. Tibby had to learn to live without her. She would be upset at first, but each day would get easier.

The crying had turned to sobs. Maddie tried to shut it out as she trudged toward the main road. Don't look back, Maddie told herself fiercely. Just keep walking. If you give in now, it'll be that much harder tomorrow.

Maddie was nearly to the road when she heard Tibby scream. Without thinking, Maddie spun around. She saw Tibby running across the yard toward her, sobbing and stumbling on the uneven ground. As the child came closer, Maddie heard Tibby mumbling something.

Maddie started walking toward Tibby. She had almost reached the girl when Tibby cried out, "Mama! Don't go!"

Maddie stopped short. *Mama.* Tibby had said *Mama.* She had talked!

The child threw herself at Maddie, wrapping her arms around Maddic's lcgs and sobbing into her skirt. "Mama," Tibby whispered in a heartbroken voice.

Maddie stooped down and pulled Tibby into her arms. With the girl's face pressed against hers, Maddie wasn't sure where Tibby's tears ended and her own began.

When Miz Colegrove answered Maddie's knock, she said, "You're late." Then she saw Tibby sitting under a

131

tree in the kitchen yard. "Told you not to bring your young'un."

"She won't be any trouble," Maddie said quickly. "She'll wait there for me and won't bother anything."

Miz Colegrove frowned. "Don't know if this'll work," she muttered. "Well, get on in here. Day's half gone as it is."

Maddie peered into rooms as Miz Colegrove led her down the center hall. With the velvet draperies drawn against the sunlight, Maddie had the impression of dark, gloomy rooms crowded with heavy pieces of furniture. And there were vases and lamps and statues on every shelf and table, Maddie noted with dismay. If the upstairs was like this, it would take her days just to dust it all.

"You can begin with the bedrooms," Miz Colegrove said as she started up the wide front stairs. For a frail little woman, she moved quickly, Maddie thought as she hurried after her. "Monday's washin' day," Miz Colegrove went on. "Tuesday's ironin', Wednesday's cleanin' . . ."

Maddie followed her down the upstairs hall. Through the open doors, she could see crowded rooms and bric-a-brac on every surface. Maddie sighed.

Miz Colegrove handed her a dustcloth and a broom. "Well, don't just stand there," the woman snapped as Maddie looked around her. "You can't leave till you finish, and I don't plan on feedin' you supper."

After a day or two, Maddie realized that working for Miz Colegrove wasn't as daunting as it had first appeared. For one thing, with the draperies drawn all the time, it was too dark to see whether the furniture had been dusted or not. And since Miz Colegrove lived alone, the weekly washing wasn't a great chore. There wasn't much ironing either, but the woman inspected each piece Maddie pressed, and if there was the tiniest crease or wrinkle in it, Maddie was told to do it over. Miz Colegrove was sharp-tongued and never smiled, but mostly she left Maddie alone. And at the end of the week, she handed Maddie a dollar.

"You got a lot to learn about ironin'," Miz Colegrove said with a frown, "but I'll teach you 'fore we're done."

Maddie stared at the dollar and grinned. "Thank you, ma'am."

Miz Colegrove just grunted.

Maddie told everybody that Tibby had spoken, but the child was slow to do it again. At suppertime, Maddie would ask, "You want another piece'a pie, Tibby?" and Tibby would nod without speaking. "What dress you wanta wear today?" Maddie would ask, and rather than tell her, Tibby would climb to the loft and pull out the blue one.

"Be patient," Mama told Maddie. "When she feels the need to speak, she will."

At school a few days later, Tibby proved that Mama was right.

Jane was teaching half the class their numbers while Maddie helped the other half with reading. Tibby sat at the edge of the reading circle, listening as each child took a turn reading aloud.

"That was very good, Letty," Maddie said. "James, you wanta try?"

The little boy took the book from Letty, but he was watching Tibby. "Why I gotta read and she don't?" he asked.

"She don't read 'cause she's a dummy," another boy said.

James snickered and soon all the children were giggling, even Pride.

Maddie gave Pride a sharp look, then stared hard at each child in turn. The giggling stopped.

"We don't call folks names in this class," Maddie said firmly. "You all understand that?"

"Yes'm," some of the children muttered. And then James said, "But that weren't callin' her a name. She *is* a dummy."

The children laughed at this. But before Maddie could respond, Tibby said with a scowl, "I'm not a dummy!"

The children stopped laughing and stared at Tibby.

"She talked," James said softly.

Pride grinned and patted Tibby on the shoulder. Tibby just scowled at them.

"You sure you don't want me to stay and help clean up?" Maddie asked Jane after class that night.

"No, you take those two on home," Jane said, nodding to where Pride and Tibby waited by the door. "Miss Tibby, you think you could say good night to me before you go?"

Tibby hung her head, looking shy.

"Another day, maybe," Jane said kindly.

"I'll come early tomorrow and light the fire," Maddie said as she and the children were leaving. "Good night, Jane."

A breeze stirred the trees and the moon cast a silver glow across the fields as they walked toward home. This was Maddie's favorite time of year. She loved those first cool days, when the air was crisp and smelled so clean, leaves crackled underfoot, and the moon seemed close enough to touch. Maddie threw back her head and gazed at the star-dusted sky. "Hello, Papa," she whispered to the North Star. She felt a moment of near-perfect peace.

After the children were in bed, Maddie sat with Mama by the fire. Mama was sewing on a winter coat for Pride.

"You gonna keep workin' for that woman?" Mama asked, not looking up from her sewing.

"For a while," Maddie said. "I'll still do all my chores here."

"I'm not worried about that," Mama said. "You've always done your share and more. I just don't see the need for you to take outside work. If it's your own money you want, you can sell eggs each week—we got more'n we need."

Before Maddie could reply, there was a soft knock on the door.

"Who'd be comin' out this late?" Mama wondered.

There was a louder knock and Maddie went to open the door. She smiled when she saw Jane standing on the porch—but the smile died instantly when she saw the state the teacher was in. "Jane?" Maddie reached out to her, but the woman stepped back.

"Jane, what happened?" Maddie whispered. Her eyes darted over the teacher's torn shirtwaist and muddy skirt. Her feet were bare and her hair—her long, lovely hair—had been cut—no, chopped!—nearly to the scalp. Tears poured down Jane's cheeks from eyes that were frighteningly vacant.

"Maddie?" Mama called as she came toward the

135

door. Then she saw the teacher. "Dear Lord," she said softly and hurried over to wrap her arms around Jane. "Maddie, fix a cup'a herb tea and get a blanket. Come on, child," she said to Jane in a soothing voice. "We're gonna take care'a you. Let's go in by the fire."

When Maddie returned with the blanket, Jane was sitting in Mama's rocker staring blankly at the fire. Tears still rolled down her cheeks.

"This'll help warm you," Mama said, draping the blanket around Jane's shoulders.

Maddie heated tea and pressed a cup of it into Jane's hands. The teacher raised the cup slowly to her lips. Her hands were shaking violently.

"Let me help," Maddie said softly. She held the cup while Jane sipped.

"The tea'll calm you," Mama said gently. "There, you're not shakin' so bad. Drink it slow, that's right."

Mama talked in that soothing way for a while, and Maddie saw the tension drain gradually from Jane's body.

"I'll get you more tea," Maddie said.

The teacher shook her head slightly. "I don't need it," she said hoarsely. She looked up, and her eyes focused on Maddie for the first time. New tears poured down her cheeks.

"You can tell us what happened if you want to," Mama said, "but you don't have to."

Jane squeezed her eyes shut. A spasm of pain contorted her face. "Men came," she whispered. "To the school." She gripped the chair arms hard. "Men with masks."

Mama patted the teacher's shoulder and dabbed at

her tears with a handkerchief. "You don't have to talk yet," Mama said.

Jane shook her head. "No. I have to tell you. They said we didn't need a school . . . niggers don't need to read and write . . . niggers don't carry parasols . . . they dragged me . . . dragged me. . . tore my clothes . . ." Jane began to cry softly, her body shaking as she covered her face with her hands.

"Hush, now," Mama said. "It's all right."

Jane's hands dropped limply into her lap. Her face looked ravaged. And her poor head with its few ragged tufts of hair made Maddie want to cry.

The teacher took a deep breath and wiped the tears away fiercely. "They dragged me outside and tied me to a tree. I thought . . ." Her lip trembled and she struggled to maintain her composure. "I thought they were going to kill me," she finished in a whisper.

Mama and Maddie's eyes met over the teacher's head. Mama just shook her head and kept on patting Jane's arm.

"They yelled terrible things," Jane said. She looked up at Maddie with the expression of a puzzled child. "Why do they hate me?" she asked.

"It's not just you," Maddie said in a tight voice. "They hate all of us."

"They said learning just gives niggers ideas," Jane said. She started to cry again. "One of them pulled my hair loose and he took out a knife and he—he cut it off." Her shoulders were shaking with sobs. "They said I was lucky this time," she said, "but if I didn't leave town, I'd be sorry."

Mama held Jane close and murmured softly to her.

Maddie walked over to the window. She stared out at the darkness for a long time, until Jane was finally quiet and Mama took her back to her own bed to sleep.

When Mama came out, closing the bedroom door behind her, Maddie said, "These people won't ever accept us, no matter what we do." As she spoke, she felt something hard and cold forming inside her.

"Maybe, one day—"

"Never!" Maddie cried. "They'll *never* stop hatin' us. If we work hard to make a good life, they say we're gettin' ideas, forgettin' our place. They don't even see us as people. We're still nothin' more'n slaves in their eyes. And that's how they mean to keep us—bowin' and scrapin' and cowerin' in the shadows."

16

All the children and their families had gathered at the Loftis cabins to say good-bye to the teacher. Jane came out of her cabin with her chin held high. Her chopped-off hair was covered with a pretty bonnet.

When Jane saw everyone standing there, she looked as though she might cry. But then she pulled herself up and forced a smile. It was a poor imitation of the warm, bright smile that Maddie had come to know. Jane looked exhausted, Maddie thought—all the energy and passion snuffed right out of her. And even though she was being kind, accepting hugs and speaking to folks as she made her way to Daniel's wagon, Maddie knew that Jane wanted nothing more than to leave this place and never come back. Maddie understood that feeling.

When Jane reached her, Maddie said, "I hate to see you leave, but I don't blame you. You're right to go."

Jane shook her head slightly. "I'm not right to go," she said in a sad voice. "I'm just not strong enough to stay."

She hugged Maddie quickly. "Take care of yourself," she said.

Maddie watched Daniel help the teacher into his wagon, where her trunks and crates of books had already been loaded. Jane waved as the wagon pulled away from the cabins, but then she turned and didn't look back.

Brother Isaac walked over to Maddie and watched the wagon until it was out of sight. "I feel bad for bringin' her here," he said.

"It's not your fault," Maddie said sharply. Then more gently, "These children needed a teacher. They still do."

Brother Isaac nodded. "Yes, they do," he said. "But I reckon they ain't gonna have one now. Less'n you'd consider stayin' on. Jane thought a lot'a you," he rushed on. "Said you wuz a born teacher. Reckon I don't have the right to ask—"

"You want me to teach the children?" Maddie asked in surprise.

"Why, sure," Brother Isaac said. "You been teachin' 'em all along, ain'tcha?"

"I was just helpin' Jane," Maddie said quickly. "And if I did fill in, I couldn't do it for long—just till spring, or summer at the latest."

A smile spread across the preacher's face. "Then you'll do it? Just till spring," he added hastily.

"I reckon I could," she said reluctantly.

"That's fine," Brother Isaac said, grabbing her hand and patting it. "That's real fine." Then his smile faded. "But should I be askin' you to take the risk?"

Maddie felt that hard, cold feeling stir inside her. "I'm not scared of a bunch'a cowards hidin' behind masks," she said fiercely. "I'll keep the school open till spring, but you have to look for somebody to take over then."

"I will," Brother Isaac said. "I surely will. Bless you, Maddie."

* * *

"I know the children need a teacher," Mama said to Maddie, "but you heard what those men said to Jane. No tellin' what they might do next time."

"I agree with Mama," Angeline said. "It's too dangerous, Maddie. The sheriff's lookin' into the attack on Jane. Wait and see what he does."

"What *can* he do?" Maddie demanded. "Jane couldn't identify the men. And even if she could, it'd be a colored woman's word against white men. They're gonna get away with it."

"Then they'll be that much more likely to lash out again," Mama said.

"So what should we do?" Maddie asked. "Not teach our children to read 'cause it makes the white folks mad? Not own land 'cause they'll say we're bein' uppity? Papa didn't fight and die so we could go on livin' like somebody's pet dog. We're free, and we gotta start *actin'* free or it won't mean a thing."

Mama stared out the window at Pride and Tibby playing in the yard. After a moment, she said, "Do what you have to, Maddie, but don't ask me not to worry."

Maddie walked over to the window. She put her arm around Mama's shoulder and they stood there together, watching the children.

That night, Maddie lay awake, unable to sleep. She kept seeing Jane's face, alight with joy and excitement when she said to Maddie, "I want to do something that matters." She saw Papa's face, too, the weariness lifting when he talked about his family's future—a future filled with hope and possibilities. Had Mama been right all those years when she'd accused him of being a

141

foolish dreamer? Had he been lying to himself when he imagined a good life for them all? Surely he must have known that white folks wouldn't give in so easily— going from master to equal overnight. But Papa had never spoken of that. All his thoughts and dreams had hinged on one thing: the end of slavery.

Well, Maddie thought sadly, slavery had ended. But *feelings* hadn't changed. Whites looked at Maddie and Jane and all the coloreds who wanted something better for themselves and their children and saw uppity, disobedient niggers. Jane had said that feelings toward colored folks weren't much different in Ohio. But Maddie couldn't let herself believe that. It had to be better than this *someplace!* And she was going to find that place.

Next morning, Maddie was taking bread out of the oven when Miz Colegrove came into the kitchen. The woman peered at the golden brown loaves and nodded.

"Looks right good," she said. "Where'd you learn to bake like that?"

"My mama was cook on the plantation," Maddie said. "She taught me."

"Nothin' better'n bread right outta the oven."

Maddie didn't say anything. She placed the bread on the windowsill to cool.

"Reckon I better cut one loaf—see how it tastes," Miz Colegrove said. "Go to the cellar and get a jar of strawberry preserves."

When Maddie came back, she saw that Miz Colegrove had placed three china plates on the table and was filling three glasses with milk.

"Call your girl in," Miz Colegrove said. "She looks like she needs some fattenin' up."

Maddie just stood there staring at the woman. She wanted Tibby inside the house? She was actually going to feed them?

"Well, you gonna call her or not?" the woman demanded. "Bread's gettin' cold."

Maddie went out to the yard, where Tibby was sitting in the grass playing with a cornshuck doll. Maddie watched her for a moment, trying to decide what to do. Tibby would love bread with strawberry preserves, but Maddie didn't want to have to feel grateful to the woman. She could feed her own family—she didn't need a white woman doing it for her.

Tibby looked up and saw Maddie.

"You wanta come inside and have some bread I baked?" Maddie asked her. "You don't have to. You can stay here if you want."

Tibby looked toward the house, thinking. Then she stood up and took Maddie's hand. "I'll come," she said to Maddie's surprise.

When they entered the kitchen, Miz Colegrove pointed to the table, where the sliced bread and glasses of milk waited. "Sit," she said.

Tibby watched Maddie sit down.

"Come on," Maddie said, indicating the chair next to her.

Tibby climbed into the chair.

Miz Colegrove sat down across from Tibby. She spread preserves on a slice of bread and placed it on Tibby's plate. "Eat," she said.

While they ate, Maddie watched Tibby. So did Miz

143

Colegrove. Tibby ate heartily, seemingly unaware of their eyes on her.

"She's a pretty little thing," Miz Colegrove said. "Daddy was a white man, I reckon."

Maddie's body tensed. She wasn't about to discuss Tibby's daddy with the woman.

"You want more milk?" Miz Colegrove asked Tibby.

Tibby nodded.

"Say please," Maddie said.

Tibby dropped her eyes and said nothing.

"Doesn't talk much, does she?" Miz Colegrove asked as she filled Tibby's glass. "Well, that's all right. Most folks run their mouths when they don't have anything to say."

Maddie frowned. Why was the woman being so agreeable? She was acting almost . . . kind. As though she liked Tibby!

Tibby sipped her milk and regarded Miz Colegrove solemnly.

The woman nodded to the cornshuck doll, which Tibby had placed beside her plate. "You like dollies?" she asked. When Tibby didn't answer, Miz Colegrove said, " 'Course you do. All little girls love dolls. My daughter Anna had a passel of 'em."

"You have a daughter?" Maddie asked before she thought.

"Had." The single word came out hard, and Maddie was sorry she'd said anything.

"Anna died," Miz Colegrove said. "Had a cholera outbreak in '32. I lost Anna and my husband the same week."

Maddie felt a twinge of pity for the old woman. "I'm sorry," she murmured.

"Long time ago now," Miz Colegrove said briskly. "You wanta see Anna's dolls?" she asked Tibby.

Tibby's face lit up. And Maddie was surprised to see something close to a smile on Miz Colegrove's thin, pale lips.

"Come on, then," the woman said.

Maddie and Tibby followed her upstairs to one of the back bedrooms. When she was cleaning the room, Maddie had thought how pretty it was. A window seat covered in faded rose-colored fabric matched the flowered carpet. The white bed covering had tiny roses embroidered on it.

Miz Colegrove went to a cupboard and opened the door. Inside was a row of small dresses in soft colors. The shelves to one side held books and toys. Several dolls sat on the top shelf.

Miz Colegrove reached for one of the dolls. It looked like the ones in the general store, although it was obviously not new.

"She called this one Mary Anne," the woman said softly, running her fingers lightly over the shiny black curls and pale pink cheeks.

Tibby stared in wonder at the doll. Seeing the longing in her eyes, Maddie felt sad. She would have loved to give Tibby a doll like this, but there was no telling how much it would cost.

Miz Colegrove sat down heavily on the window seat. She was still stroking the doll's face. "Anna had black curls," the woman said. "Her papa called her 'my pretty.' "

Miz Colegrove seemed to have forgotten that Maddie and Tibby were there. Maddie took Tibby's hand and led her quietly to the door. The woman was still caressing the doll and murmuring, "My pretty, my pretty girl."

When it was nearly time to leave for school, Maddie went to the loft and opened a small, battered trunk at the foot of her mattress. Inside were the treasures she had brought with her from the island.

She took out each item, one at a time. The gray cloak she'd gotten that first Christmas from the missionary barrel. A horsehair bracelet that Sula Jackson had shown her how to make. A giant pine cone that she and Zebedee had found in the woods. Some shells they had picked up on the beach. And a book of poems by Walt Whitman.

Maddie drew out the book and looked at it. *Leaves of Grass* was written in gold on the green leather binding. That Christmas on the island, Sergeant Taylor had taken the book from the missionary barrel and handed it to Maddie. "Just the thing for the camp's teacher," he'd said.

It was the first book Maddie had ever owned—the most wonderful gift anyone had ever given her. She had read it over and over during their years on the island. She had read Papa's favorite poem aloud to him more times than she could count. But since they'd left the island, she hadn't looked at the book again. She thought of it often, tucked away safely in the trunk, but she hadn't wanted to read from it or even see it. Because it reminded her of that joyous Christmas— their first Christmas of freedom. They had been so happy then, so filled with hopes and dreams. And Papa's eyes had glowed with excitement when she read

that one poem to him. He had asked to hear it often—
the last time, the night before he left for the war.

Maddie opened the book to Papa's poem. She looked
at the print on the page and slowly began to read.

> *Afoot and light-hearted I take to the open road,*
> *Healthy, free, the world before me,*
> *The long brown path before me leading wherever I*
>   *choose.*

Leading wherever I choose. The poem was a lie. There
was no choosing for colored folks. The choices had
already been made for them. How could Mama go on
hoping that things would get better, that these people
would ever change? They'd killed Papa. They'd taken
away her family's home on the island. They'd tried
to shut down the school. And their anger just kept
growing.

Maddie closed the book and put it back into the
trunk, out of sight.

17

The weather turned from cool to cold in December. Maddie pulled the gray wool cloak from the trunk and draped it over Tibby's shoulders. It fell nearly to Tibby's feet, but Tibby loved it. She ran around the house with the cloak billowing behind her.

A few days before Christmas Angeline and Ruth came to help Mama with the baking. Maddie was sewing on a rag doll for Tibby. The hair was made from yellow yarn and the eyes were dark brown buttons from one of Mama's old dresses. Maddie had used a scrap from Tibby's blue calico dress to make a matching dress for the doll.

Maddie looked up from her sewing and sniffed the air. "That apple cake I smell?"

"It is." Angeline placed the rich brown cake on the table beside the sweet potato pies. "Maddie, you reckon you could sew up a doll like that for Elizabeth?" she asked. "I haven't had time for presents."

"Angeline, you didn't bring the pecans," Mama said. "Christmas won't be Christmas without pecan pies."

"And we gotta have pumpkin pie," Ruth added.

"And cracklin' bread," Angeline said.

"The pecans," Mama demanded, frowning at Angeline.

"I'll bring 'em tomorrow," Angeline said. "We can't do ever'thing in one day, Mama."

"And we can't put ever'thing off till the last minute," Mama insisted. "There's so much to do."

Maddie smiled to herself as she sewed. Getting ready for Christmas had always been an exciting time, even back on the plantation. And nobody loved the hurry and scurry of getting ready better than Mama. Even when she worked in the Big House from dawn to dark, Mama had found time to clean and bake and make presents for her family. And she'd always fretted that she'd never be ready by Christmas.

On Christmas Eve night, Maddie set the table while Mama and Angeline finished cooking supper. Mama had just set the ham on the table when Pride came running in, yelling, "Daniel's wagon's comin' up the road!"

Mama had invited their friends for Christmas Eve supper. Ruth and Zebedee, Daniel and William, Brother Isaac, and Reba and Tom and their children. Soon the house was filled with laughter. And memories of other Christmases.

"Remember our first Christmas on the island?" Angeline asked during supper. "We were livin' in that old tent and it smelled like a wet dog."

Mama smiled. "That was a happy Christmas," she said.

"Remember the fiddle music?" Zebedee asked Maddie. "You wanted me to dance with you."

"And you wouldn't," Maddie retorted.

"Lucky for you!" Zebedee said. "I'd have just stomped your feet."

"That was when you got the book of poems,"

149

Angeline said to Maddie. "Where is that book? I haven't seen it in a long time."

"I still have it," Maddie said.

After supper, Daniel pulled out his harmonica and began to play. They all sang along.

> *There's a star in the East on Christmas morn,*
> *Rise up shepherds and follow.*
> *It'll lead to the place where the savior's born,*
> *Rise up shepherds and follow.*

While they were singing, Maddie noticed William sitting off to himself by the door. He was staring at the floor and not singing.

She heard Jubal bark. William lifted his head and Maddie looked away. But out of the corner of her eye, she saw him stand and open the door. As the door closed silently behind him, Maddie stood up and followed.

When she went out to the front porch, William had already disappeared into the darkness. Maddie walked down the steps. She stopped when she heard hushed voices in the yard, then the crackling of leaves underfoot as William and someone else walked toward the road.

The door opened and Zebedee came outside.

"What you doin' out here in the cold?" he asked.

"William left," Maddie said softly. "Heard him talkin' to somebody. Ben probably. You figger they're up to somethin'?"

Zebedee sighed. "I'll go see."

"Let's tell Daniel," Maddie said. "I don't want you goin' alone."

"No need to worry him and Ruth." Zebedee patted Maddie's arm. "You go inside. I can handle it."

Maddie watched him leave. Jubal came out of the darkness and leaned against her. Maddie stroked his head. Then she returned reluctantly to the house.

The music had gotten more lively. They sang "Camptown Races" and "Fare You Well, Fare You Well." When Ruth asked between songs if anyone had seen Zeb, Maddie said he'd gone for a walk. "William go with him?" Ruth asked, and Maddie nodded. Ruth looked puzzled, but then Daniel began to play "Oh! Susanna" and Ruth joined in the singing.

An hour passed. Angeline and Royall were dancing. Pride and Tibby and the Spivey children were whirling around the room, bumping into each other and giggling.

Maddie watched the door. What could be keeping Zebedee? Where had William and Ben gone? She thought several times about telling Daniel, but Zeb had said he could handle it.

It was much later when Daniel finally put his harmonica away. "I can't blow another note," he said with a grin.

"We best be gettin' on home," Reba said.

"It's late," Daniel agreed.

"But Zeb and William aren't back," Ruth said.

"Maybe they walked home," Mama said.

"Why would they do that?" Ruth asked. She looked worried.

Maddie was about to tell them why Zebedee had left when she heard someone on the porch. The door opened and Zeb came in.

"We wuz wonderin' . . ." Ruth started, but the rest of the words died on her lips.

One look at his face and they all knew something was wrong. Very wrong.

"Zeb, what is it?" Maddie asked.

Zebedee looked from her to Ruth and Daniel. "I got William outside."

Ruth started for the door.

"He's hurt," Zeb said.

Maddie lit a lantern and followed the others outside. William was slumped on the steps, with Daniel and Ruth and Brother Isaac bent over him. Zebedee and the others looked on from the porch.

When the light from the lantern fell on William, Maddie could see a dark stain across the front of his shirt. Then she saw the streak of red on Ruth's dress where she had leaned against him.

"This boy's been shot," Brother Isaac said.

William whimpered. He looked like he was in a lot of pain. "I didn't mean it," he said softly. Then he began to cry.

"Bring him inside," Mama said. "Angeline, there's clean rags in the storeroom. And heat some water."

Daniel and Brother Isaac carried William into the house. They put him down on the floor in front of the fire. Mama opened his shirt, and they could see a blood-soaked bandage stuck to his shoulder.

"Oh, no," Ruth whispered. She sat down beside William and stroked his face.

"I tried to stop the bleedin'," Zeb said. "But I had to get him outta there."

"Outta where?" Daniel asked.

"Mister Gentry's barn."

Daniel's head jerked up. "What happened, Zeb?"

Angeline had brought clean cloths and a basin of water. Mama started to bathe the wound. William cried out at the touch of the cloth.

"Ben come here to get William," Zebedee said. "I followed 'em to the Gentry place. I shoulda stopped 'em 'fore they got to the barn—"

"Can't worry over that now," Daniel said sharply, his eyes fixed on William's face.

"The house wuz dark like ever'body wuz in bed," Zebedee went on. "I seen William and Ben go around the house, then duck into the barn. I went after 'em, but it was too dark inside to see anything. Then Ben lit a lantern and opened a stall door. He led one'a the horses out and started to put a bridle on it. That's when I said, 'What you think you're doin'?' "

"All we wanted was to leave here," William said, his face contorted with pain. "Needed horses to go out West."

"You wuz stealin' horses?" Daniel shook his head in disbelief. "How could you be so stupid?"

William began to cry again.

"Hush," Ruth said softly, still stroking his face.

Daniel looked up at Zebedee. "How'd he get shot?"

" 'Bout that time, the barn door opened," Zebedee said. "It was Mister Gentry. He had a rifle. He looked at Ben with his horse, then at me. Said to me, 'I knowed you wuz nothin' but trouble. Stealin' my horses'll get you a rope around the neck.' "

William groaned. "I don't wanta hang. Daniel"—he grabbed the front of Daniel's jacket—"Help me, Daniel. You gotta help me."

Zebedee sat down wearily on the floor. "William

153

started runnin' for the back door. Mister Gentry yelled for him to stop. William turned around and Gentry fired at him. William cried out and Mister Gentry started toward him. That's when Ben come up behind Gentry with a shovel and hit him on the head with it. Mister Gentry dropped the rifle and fell to the floor. He didn't move."

"Dear Lord," Ruth muttered. "Ben killed him?"

"No, he wuz still alive," Zebedee said quickly. "I put my head on his chest and he wuz breathin'."

"Ben run out on me," William said softly. "Jumped on that horse and took off."

"Reckon he's in the next county by now," Zebedee said. "I didn't know what else to do but bring William here."

"You did right," Mama said. "I think the bleedin's stopped. Looks like the bullet went clean through."

"Mister Gentry recognized you, Zeb," Maddie said. "When he comes to, he'll have the sheriff lookin' for you."

"Zebedee didn't do nothin' wrong," Ruth said, her eyes filled with fear.

"Mister Gentry won't believe that," Daniel said.

"These boys gotta leave," Brother Isaac said. "Get outta town now."

"No!" Ruth said.

"He's right," Daniel told her. "Ben and William wuz stealin' a horse, and Ben attacked Gentry. He's got the law on his side."

"Ain't no way they'd get a fair trial," Brother Isaac said. "If the men in this town even waited for the judge to get here. Might decide to try 'em themselves."

Ruth began to cry. Maddie sat down beside her and

held her. But her eyes were on Zebedee. He looked dazed.

"Don't have much time." Daniel stood up and reached into his pocket. "I got a little money. I'll drive Zeb and William to the train at Durham Station. We'll buy 'em tickets for as far away as this'll take 'em."

"You think nobody's gonna question a colored boy gettin' on a train when he's been shot?" Mama asked.

"He'll have to act like he hasn't been shot," Daniel said.

"I'll get him one'a my shirts," Royall said, starting for the door.

"Sit up," Daniel said to William.

William tried, then fell back with a moan.

"You do what I say," Daniel said sharply. "Now sit up!"

William sat up with Mama and Ruth helping him. Daniel pulled him to his feet. Tears streamed down William's face and he moaned again.

"Straighten up," Daniel said. "For once in your life, William, show some gumption!"

Ruth looked at Zebedee. "I'm goin', too," she said.

Zebedee shook his head. "No, you ain't."

"I'm goin'," Ruth said. "You don't have no say in this."

"But where?" Angeline asked.

"Ohio," Maddie said. "I have Jane's address in Oberlin. In Ohio, you'll have a chance to live like human bein's."

"Won't it cost a lot to get there?" Ruth asked.

"I got money," Mama said. She went to the storeroom and came out carrying a jar.

"But if they don't find Ben and William and me, they might do somethin' to the rest'a you," Zebedee said.

"It's the three'a you they'll want," Brother Isaac said. "But I'll go talk to Mister Loftis once you're gone. He'll keep Mister Gentry from doin' somethin' crazy."

Mama handed the jar of money to Zebedee. He started to protest, but she wouldn't hear it. "You worked as hard as any of us for this," she said. "Maddie, come help me get some food ready."

Maddie followed Mama into the storeroom. She was wrapping sliced ham in a cloth when Mama said, "It's you always had your heart set on goin' north. Here's your chance, daughter."

Maddie's eyes met Mama's. Could she really mean that Maddie should go with them?

Mama touched Maddie's face lightly. "It's now or later, I reckon," she said. "So go pack your things. But hurry! You gotta leave soon."

Maddie hugged Mama hard, her heart racing with excitement. And fear. She pulled away and searched Mama's face. "But you may need me when they come lookin' for Zeb."

"You heard Brother Isaac," Mama said. "They don't want us. Now, hurry, child."

Maddie went into the front room. Royall was back. He was helping Daniel take off William's blood-soaked shirt and jacket. Zebedee was talking quietly to Pride. Angeline was holding Elizabeth on one knee and Tibby on the other. When Tibby saw Maddie, she ran to her.

Maddie hugged the child. "You stay here with Angeline," she said. "I'll be back in a minute."

Maddie climbed the ladder to the loft. She rolled her second-best dress and a change of underthings up in a blanket. Then she opened the trunk. She took out the sheet of paper with Jane's address written on it and the six dollars she'd saved, put them in the pocket of her skirt, and closed the trunk lid. Then she remembered something. She knew she couldn't take all her treasures, but surely she could take just one. Maddie opened the trunk lid again and reached for the book.

Soon she would be on her way to Ohio. Away from this place and all the people who hated her. It was hard now that the time had come, but Mama had told her to go. Maybe later, when Maddie was settled and had a job, she'd be able to talk Mama into coming north. For a visit, at least. And she could bring Tibby and Pride. Maybe Angeline and Royall would come, too.

Maddie sat looking at the book. *Afoot and light-hearted I take to the open road.* "Well, Papa, I'm goin'," Maddie whispered. Wasn't this what you wanted for me? The chance to make up my own mind? To go where I want? But choices were hard, Maddie thought. Why did they have to be so hard?

They were waiting for her when she came downstairs. Zebedee was grinning. "Your mama sez you're comin' with us."

Mama was holding Tibby. When Maddie looked at her, Mama nodded. Her expression seemed to say, *Go, Maddie. Follow your dream.* Tibby was looking first at Maddie, then at Mama, as though trying to figure out what was happening. Her eyes were huge in her tiny face. She's so little, Maddie thought. She's lost so much.

Maddie reached into her pocket and handed Zeb the money and Jane's address. She gave Ruth the bundle of clothing. "I can't go," she said.

Zebedee's face fell. "But you wuz the one that always wanted to go north."

"I did," Maddie said. "But I can't."

"You sure?" Mama asked in a quiet voice.

Maddie nodded, but she wasn't *sure* about anything anymore. She just knew that she couldn't leave. Not now. Not yet.

Maddie handed the book of poems to Zebedee. "Take this. And when you look at it, remember the island, and Papa. And me," she said.

Zebedee stared at the book. Then he wrapped his arms around Maddie and squeezed her hard. "I'll take it," he said softly, "but I don't need nothin' to remind me'a you, Maddie Henry."

Then Ruth was hugging her. "I won't say good-bye," Ruth said. She pulled away and hurried out the door.

"Time to go," Daniel told them.

Royall and Brother Isaac helped William walk to the door. Maddie and Zebedee followed.

As Royall and Brother Isaac lifted William into the wagon, Zebedee turned to Maddie. He was trying to smile, but Maddie had never seen him look so sad. "I'll keep the book for you—but just till I see you again," he said. Then he ran down the steps and climbed into the wagon bed.

Daniel came out carrying a bundle of food. "Don't worry," he said to Maddie. "I'll keep him safe."

Maddie watched Daniel climb into the wagon and tap the mules lightly with the reins. "And keep yourself safe," she called to him.

Daniel raised his hand and nodded. Then the wagon moved slowly into darkness.

Later, when the horses came pounding down the

158

road and up to the house, Mister Loftis was sitting on the porch. He had a rifle with him, but he didn't have to use it.

Maddie sat in Mama's rocker in the dark. She stayed there long after the men had ridden away and Mister Loftis had gone home, with Tibby asleep in her arms.

18

Maddie, Angeline, and Royall went to the fields at daybreak one sunny morning. They had planted the corn early in the spring and now, in late May, it was a foot high and needed hoeing.

Mama was on the porch shelling the first peas from her garden and watching Elizabeth as the child toddled across the yard. Pride and Tibby were supposed to be weeding the kitchen garden. But when Maddie looked up from her work, she saw Pride down by the pond and Tibby and Jubal running up the hill. Maddie smiled, remembering herself at that age and how often she had sneaked away from the Big House to play with the stable cats or meet Papa when he came in from the fields. How Mama had scolded her!

It had been a quiet spring. So quiet that Maddie could sometimes believe that Mama was right, that the town was beginning to accept them. She knew that Mister Gentry would never forgive them—only Mister Loftis had kept him from venting his rage on them last Christmas. And the storekeeper was more surly than ever when they went to the store to shop. But there had been no more night riders or attacks at the school. Daniel and Brother Isaac and some of the other men took turns standing watch at the school, just in case, but no one had bothered them again.

And there were some people who were kind. When one of the mules had died during planting, Amos Crowe, the blacksmith, had sold Royall a young mule for much less than they'd expected to pay. And Mister Loftis had his workers fix up the barn where they met for church and school. And even Miz Colegrove was less cranky. She always gave Tibby cookies or a piece of pie on baking day, and right after Christmas she took a wrapped gift outside to Tibby and handed it to her. Tibby looked puzzled until Miz Colegrove said, "It's a late Christmas present. Open it." Tibby tore into the tissue paper with glee; and then, when she saw what the package contained, she sat there staring at it in disbelief. It was the doll, Mary Anne, with her shiny black curls and soft pink cheeks.

"Miz Colegrove, Tibby can't take your daughter's doll," Maddie had said, confused and troubled by the woman's generosity.

"I reckon she can if I want her to have it," the woman had said sharply. Then, as they'd watched Tibby lift the doll gently from the wrappings and cradle it in her arms, Miz Colegrove had said, "And I want her to have it."

But if Maddie had cause to be hopeful, she also had reason to be wary. She had seen with her own eyes the harm that people's bitterness could cause. And she knew that the old ways of thinking and acting wouldn't change overnight. *We're free, Papa, but we still have a ways to go.*

When Daniel's wagon pulled up that morning, everybody waved, then went back to work—they knew it was Maddie he had come to see, as he did frequently these days. Maddie left the field, taking off her bonnet and wiping her face, as she walked to meet him.

161

Daniel was smiling. "Got a letter from Ruth," he said. "She's writin' good now. Says the teachers at the school she and Zeb goes to is helpin' him get ready for college. There's even folks that'll pay for it if he does good on some test."

"Zeb wrote me about it," Maddie said. She looked pleased and proud. "Imagine, our little Zeb goin' to college. He could become a doctor or a lawyer."

"Ruth says he wants to teach. Maybe come back to North Carolina."

Maddie smiled. Dreams, she thought. They had a way of taking hold when you least expected it. "Did Ruth say anything about William?" she asked.

"He's in school, but he's not much interested in book learnin'. And he's still got that temper." Daniel frowned. "Ruth says he'll find his way one day. Don't reckon she'll ever give up on that boy."

"She shouldn't," Maddie said. "And neither should you."

They were walking away from the house toward the open fields. The tall grass was pale silver-green, still glistening with morning dew. Maddie took off her shoes, enjoying the feel of the damp earth against her bare feet.

"Ruth asked about you," Daniel said. "She says Zebedee worries 'cause he's the one in Ohio goin' to school, when it wuz you that wanted to go so bad."

Maddie nodded. "He says that in all his letters, and I tell him it's all right. I'm fine."

Daniel studied her face. "*Are* you fine, Maddie? You don't wish you'd gone with 'em?"

Maddie looked out over the fields as she thought about his question. Weren't there times when she envied Ruth and Zebedee? When she wished *she* was the one going to college? But if she weren't here, who would keep the school going? Who would help Pride with his cipherin'? Who would work with Tibby to make her talk? Maddie looked at Tibby now, standing very still on the crest of the hill, her head thrown back to watch an eagle circling overhead. The wind ruffled Tibby's yellow hair, and she raised a hand to brush it out of her eyes. There was a look of wonder on her face as she watched the bird glide across the sky. Tibby was strong now, Maddie thought. She had left the shadows behind.

Maddie turned back to Daniel. "I still wanta go north," she said. "And I *will* someday. But right now, this is where I belong."

The worried look melted from Daniel's face. "Well, I'm mighty glad you stayed," he said softly and reached for her hand. "And who's to say? Maybe someday I'll go north with you."

And maybe someday, Maddie thought, she would tell Daniel what Zebedee had taught her: that dreams aren't worth much if you don't have somebody to share them with.

Just then, Tibby looked down the hill and saw Maddie and Daniel standing there. A smile spread across her face and she waved. Then she was sprinting through the tall grass toward them, her yellow hair flying behind her, the dog barking at her heels. Tibby was laughing when she reached the bottom of the hill. And running free.

About the Author

SANDRA FORRESTER wrote this book to answer her own questions about where the Henrys would go after they gained their freedom in *Sound the Jubilee.* She says, "Their most cherished dream had come true, but the reality of freedom was harsh. If a young reader comes away from this book wondering why things haven't changed more than they have, I will be happy."

Sandra Forrester lives in Durham, North Carolina. She is a management analyst and recently obtained her master's degree in library and information studies. Her first book, *Sound the Jubilee,* was a Notable Trade Book in the Field of Social Studies.